I0598515

TEASE

TEMPTATION SERIES BOOK TWO

EVELYN BLOOM

EK PUBLISHING INC.

Edited by
L. Nunn Editing

Cover Art by
EK Designs

TEASE

Tristan isn't stupid… sleeping with the boss is an epic way to get fired.

Luckily, it's nearly impossible to flirt with Shepherd. His boss hates him so much he can barely tolerate looking Tristan in the eye.

That doesn't stop Tristan from fantasizing about all the delicious things he wants to do to Shepherd.

Hiring Tristan was a mistake. Chalk it up to Shepherd's poor judgment.

Now it's taking every last shred of his control to keep his hands off of Tristan. And no matter how sexy Tristan is, sleeping with an employee is dangerous business.

When an accident draws Tristan into Shepherd's personal life, they can't deny their attraction.

As they grow closer, the line between work life and personal life blurs.

But will Tristan's past and the unhealthy hold his family has over him ruin their budding relationship?

CHAPTER 1

Tristan

"Shepherd's gonna kill him."

"He's not gonna kill him. He's gonna *fire* him, but he won't kill him."

I stared at the copy of the invoice in my hand, my stomach queasy and my mind already halfway to packing up my shit. Behind me, Roger and Gurdeep continued to squabble about whether Shepherd would kill me or fire me.

My money was on both. First, Shepherd would fire me, then he'd kill me.

"I'm really sorry, Tristan." Marybeth looked as nauseated as I felt.

"It's not your fault," I said. "I drew up the invoice."

"Yeah, but I thought it seemed too low when I was ringing it through for the customer. I should have double checked with you." The pretty brunette looked close to tears.

I shook my head. "It's not your job to double check my work."

"I'd better get back," Marybeth said. "I can't hear the phone out here."

She left the bay, walking past the two cars currently on the lifts and the long counter of tools to get to the side door that led into the reception area.

"Maybe," Gurdeep said, "Shepherd will just beat the shit out of Tristan. I mean, he was a boxer back in the day, right? They solve shit with their fists, yeah?"

"He hasn't boxed in over a decade," Roger said.

"Yeah, but he still works out at the boxing gym over on Mayhill," Gurdeep said. "Plus, it's not like he's let himself go or anything. The guy's solid muscle."

"Doesn't mean he's gonna beat the shit out of Tristan," Roger said with a disgusted snort. He'd been working at Shepherd's shop since Shepherd first opened the garage and, much like Shepherd, he didn't suffer any fools. "Fuck, Gurdeep, are you high today? Shepherd runs a respectable business. He's not gonna beat up an employee."

Roger turned his gaze to me. "But you are gonna get fired."

I grimaced and my hand crumpled up the edge of the invoice when Shepherd's deep voice said, "Why am I firing you?"

I turned, staring uneasily at Shepherd as Roger and Gurdeep suddenly found shit to do on the far side of the bay. Shepherd had walked in through the open door of the bay and was holding a brown paper bag with the words 'The Vigilant Vegan" imprinted on the side. His t-shirt was tight across his broad chest, his jeans clung to his thick thighs, and, like usual, he had a two-day growth of dark hair on his jaw. The man always had the perfect damn amount of stubble.

Normally, I would be hard-pressed to look away from that stubble, to stop imagining what it might feel like brushing against certain sensitive spots on my body, but right now? At this moment, my usual urge to lust after my boss like a horny llama had disappeared. And all it took was the certainty that I was about to lose my damn job.

"We can talk after you eat lunch," I said. Partly because I didn't want to ruin Shepherd's lunch, and partly because maybe if I had even half an hour more, I'd come up with a convincing argument for why Shepherd shouldn't fire me.

Not a chance, buddy. You're so losing your job today.

Shepherd studied me before crooking his head at his office. "Talk to me while I'm eating."

He turned and headed toward the small hole in the wall that functioned as his office. It had two doors, one accessed through reception, just past the bathroom and storage closet, and the other door leading straight into the bay.

My stomach churning up bile, I followed Shepherd across the bay, picking my way past the third empty lift, the diagnostic equipment lined up neatly against the wall, and the tools from Roger's toolbox that he'd left scattered on the floor.

"Roger, pick up your fucking tools before I toss them in the dumpster," Shepherd said as I stepped over them.

"You got it, boss," Roger said. Wiping at the grease on his fingers, Roger ambled over to the toolbox, giving me a sympathetic look as he squatted to pick up the wrenches.

My back sweating, I followed Shepherd into the office.

"Close the door." Shepherd sat down behind his desk and cleared a space free of the piles of work orders that always seemed to cover his desk. Shepherd's office was a tornado of car parts, tools, paperwork, and... honestly, he could have had anything hidden under all the papers and tools - holy shit, was that a Barbie doll? - piled on the floor surrounding his desk. I had an idea that the last time Shepherd cleaned his office or filed anything was a decade ago when the shop first opened.

I shut the door, dimming the whir of the oscillating fans on the wall in the bay, Roger's whistling, and the idling engine of the car Gurdeep had just pulled into the empty spot in the bay. Still holding the invoice in my hand, I sat in the rusted folding chair in front of Shepherd's desk. Shepherd pulled a sandwich out of the bag. From the looks of it, it was the Vigilant Vegan's rainbow veggie sandwich.

I felt a small pang of regret. Before I'd quit the family business, the Vigilant Vegan was one of my favourite restaurants, their rainbow veggie sandwich one of my go-to's for ordering. Unfortunately, my eating-out budget had dried up significantly in the last few years.

"Tell me why I'm firing you," Shepherd said, then bit into his sandwich.

The scent of the restaurant's special – *delicious* – sauce drifted to me. Normally I'd be salivating at this point. My total lack of hunger only hammered down the reality that while I could pretend to be hopeful, I knew I was about to be fired.

Christ. I was only halfway through my apprenticeship, and I was getting fired from my first job. I'd never find another shop to take me on as an apprentice. My new career was over before it even started.

Shepherd stared pointedly at me as he chewed.

I cleared my throat. "I invoiced Trevor Warner incorrectly. Forgot to add on some stuff. He paid and left before I realized my mistake."

Now the sweat was popping up on my forehead. Shepherd took another bite of his sandwich, chewed, and swallowed. "How much did you forget to bill?"

"A significant amount," I said.

Shepherd eyed me over the sandwich. "How significant?"

Afraid I'd barf if I said anything else, I handed over the now wrinkled and slightly damp invoice copy before wiping my sweaty palms on my coveralls. I watched Shepherd's face as he read over the invoice. To my surprise, the anger I expected to wash over Shepherd's face didn't appear.

Afraid Shepherd hadn't realized what I forgot to bill, I said, "I missed the diagnostic fee and -"

"Your labour costs. I can read," Shepherd said.

He set the sandwich down on the paper wrapper and opened the bottle of water sitting on his desk. He took a drink and then leaned back in his chair, staring steadily at me. "What were you doing when you were invoicing that caused you to make such a stupid mistake?"

I winced, but what was I expecting? It was a stupid mistake. What kind of asshole forgot to bill for their time? This might be my first job as a mechanic, but I'd been working here for over six months now. I had no fucking excuse.

Sure you do. You were daydreaming about what it might be like to have Shepherd bend you over his desk and fuck you. Remember?

Dull heat climbed up my neck. I cleared my throat again as Shepherd continued to stare at me. He was waiting for an answer, but somehow I didn't think admitting that I was thinking about being fucked by him, would help save my job.

Might as well admit it, your ass is fired either way.

My inner voice was probably right, but, not including my best friend Will, I would take my inappropriate crush on my boss to my grave before I admitted it to anyone.

"I have no excuse," I said. "My head obviously wasn't in the game that day. I apologize for making such a large error."

Shepherd stared at his half-eaten sandwich. Feeling

weirdly guilty for ruining the man's appetite – which was hilarious considering I'd just admitted to causing the loss of a truly horrifying large amount of money for Shepherd – I said, "I'll pack my tools and be out of here in half an hour. I know this sounds stupid now, but I'd like to say thank you for giving me a chance. It can be hard to find work as an apprentice, and I truly appreciate you hiring me."

Shepherd continued to stare at me. I was getting the distinct 'bug pinned to a wall' feeling. I squirmed in the chair and started to stand. Shepherd scowled. "Sit down, Tristan."

The sound of my name coming from Shepherd's perfect lips usually got my motor running. But right now, the disappointment stamped into the sound of my name only soured my stomach even more.

I sank back into my chair, my stomach a tight knot of anxiety and the sweat sliding down my temples despite the coolness of the office. It wasn't just that I had fucked up in front of my crush, it was fucking up in general. I was a man who took pride in my work, and the fact that I'd made such a colossal fuck up ate at my stomach lining like poisonous venom.

"I could fire you." Shepherd's gorgeous blue eyes were searing into my damn soul. "But firing you wouldn't get back the money you cost me, would it?"

"No." Feeling even worse than I did two minutes ago, I said, "But I can't afford to pay back the money I lost you, at least not right away. Give me a month – two at the max – and I'll get you the money I owe you."

"A month or two," Shepherd repeated.

Shame making that dull heat travel up to my cheeks, I said, "If you don't fire me, I'll still need to get a second job. But I'll pay interest on the money I owe you, if you'll give me the extra time to pay you back."

"You get Sundays and Mondays off," Shepherd said. "Most shops in this town aren't open on Sunday. You think another mechanic will hire you for Mondays only?"

I shook my head. "No, I'll work in the evenings after I'm finished here."

"Doing what?"

I had no idea why Shepherd was interrogating me on what exactly I would do for part-time work. At this point, I'd sell blow jobs at the corner of Seventh and Main, if it meant I kept my damn job. The town wasn't exactly flush with mechanic jobs, and it had been luck and knowing the right person at the right time that even landed me this job at Shepherd's shop. I was just scraping by as it was, and if I lost this job, I was fucked. I'd lose my damn apartment and be begging Will to let me crash on his couch.

Don't forget the look on your father's face when you fail. Do you think he'll tell you, "I told you so" himself, or hire a choir to sing it to you? My money's on the choir.

"McDonald's down the street is looking to hire for the overnight cleaning crew. I saw the sign as I was driving to work this morning," I said.

"So, you'll work at a fucking fast food joint all night, then come in and work on cars here at the shop. When are you going to sleep?" Shepherd took another bite of his sandwich.

"I don't need much sleep," I said. Not true, but I'd rather die of sleep deprivation then have my father see me failing.

Shepherd rolled his eyes. "You work at another job all night and then come into the shop, the only thing that'll happen is you fuck up even worse. You'll either completely wreck a customer's car or get yourself killed because you're too fucking tired to concentrate."

"I won't," I said.

"Bull fucking shit," Shepherd said bluntly. "The way I see

it, you owe me about a week's worth of pay, does that sound fair to you?"

"Yes," I said.

"My options are to fire you, give you a payment plan option where you fucking kill yourself trying to pay back what you owe me, or I dock your pay every week until the amount is paid off."

I clenched my jaw. With the money I sent to my father every month, if Shepherd docked my pay, I'd still be looking for a second job.

"But I'm guessing if I dock your pay, you'll have to find a second job anyway. Is that right?" Shepherd said.

"Yeah," I said. I wanted to defend myself, wanted to convince Shepherd that I wasn't living paycheque to paycheque because of poor money management skills, but I resisted the urge. Shepherd wouldn't give one fuck why I needed every dollar I got from my paycheque.

Shepherd leaned back in his chair, tapping the cap from the water bottle on the armrest. I told myself not to look at his abs perfectly accented by the tightness of his shirt but snuck a peek anyway. Of course, this was going to be the last time I ever got to see the perfection that was Shepherd's face and body, so maybe just going ahead and blatantly ogling him was the route to take.

Before I could really humiliate myself and drop my gaze to the prominent bulge hidden behind his jeans, Shepherd said, "I'll offer a fourth option, if you're interested?"

I tore my gaze away from his wide chest. "I'm interested."

"It's not going to be enjoyable," Shepherd said.

My wild and inappropriate hope that maybe Shepherd would demand the money I owed him in the form of me on my knees behind his desk with his thick cock deep inside my mouth once a day for the next six months, died a quick death.

You don't know that his cock is thick.

It was. A man Shepherd's size would have a thick cock. One that would stretch me in all the right fucking ways while that callused hand of his worked my dick and –

"Are you even fucking listening?" Shepherd said.

I snapped back to attention. "Sorry. Tell me."

"You clean up my office. You sort through everything, put it in the shop where it belongs, and," he waved vaguely in the direction of the biggest pile of papers, "do the filing. On your own time, not during working hours. You can work in the evenings or come in on Sundays."

Relief and gratitude washed over me in a tidal wave. Was Shepherd seriously going to let me keep my job in exchange for cleaning up his small office? "Seriously? All I have to do is clean up your office? That doesn't seem like it covers the cost."

Shut up, you idiot!

Shepherd's face almost cracked a smile. "I've got paper-work in here I haven't filed in a fucking decade. Trust me, it'll cover the cost."

I wiped my sweaty palm on my coveralls, stood, and offered my hand to Shepherd. "It's a deal."

He shook my hand. Now that I was no longer wondering how big of a cardboard box I'd need for my new alley living arrangements, the slide of his callused palm against mine made my dick twitch.

Shepherd dropped my hand and feeling weirdly guilty about my lust for him, I said, "I'll get started on your office tonight after work."

I was supposed to have dinner with Will and his new boyfriend, Ian, but I'd cancel. Will would understand.

He shook his head. "It's Saturday. You can start next week."

"I'm good to work on it tonight."

"I heard you talking to Gurdeep this morning about your plans after work," he said. "Next week is fine."

"Thanks, Shepherd. I really appreciate the second chance."

"Don't fuck up again."

"I won't," I said.

"Good. Get out of here," he said. "Jack texted me earlier. The Aston broke down again, and he's having it towed over here this afternoon. You're working on it. I fucking told him not to buy that piece of shit, but you fucking slap the word vintage on it, and Jack's gotta have it, doesn't matter what condition it's in."

I laughed, too loud and too long, but I was pretty fucking giddy at not losing my job and becoming the failure my father believed me to be.

Shepherd made a flicking motion with his hand toward the door. Figuring I should get out while the getting out was good, I turned and picked my way through the piles of stuff to the door.

CHAPTER 2

Shepherd

I watched Tristan's delectable ass leave my office, my dick half-hard just like it always was whenever I was around my newest employee. I waited until the door was closed before reaching down and adjusting myself, trying to ease some of the pressure.

I shoved the last bite of my sandwich into my mouth. Fuck, I should have fired Tristan. I knew it. He knew it. Everyone in the fucking shop knew it.

So, why didn't you?

Because I knew what it was like to fuck up royally at a new job.

Because I was pretty sure the guy would end up homeless if I fired him.

Because I wouldn't get to see him every day if I fired him.

The last reason was the real truth of the matter. I wasn't too stupid or bullheaded to realize that, and it sent a thread of disquiet down my back. Lusting after an employee was a temptation I neither wanted nor needed. Tristan screwing up was the perfect excuse to fire him and end my temptation.

But instead, I was keeping him on, and even worse, he'd be in my office on a regular basis.

Your office does need to be cleaned. It's a fucking fire hazard.

That was true, but I didn't need Tristan's scent in here every damn day, driving me to distraction. The image of his dark eyes with their ridiculously long lashes popped into my head on a regular basis. I'd jacked off more than once wondering what his lean body looked like when it wasn't covered up by clothing. I was doing nothing but torturing myself by letting him into my office. I already spent a good portion of every day fantasizing about what it would be like to strip Tristan naked, bend him over my desk, and fuck him.

My dick went from half-mast to fully hard, and I grunted in annoyance before finishing off the rest of my water. I really should have fired him.

My phone rang and I dug it out of my pocket, glancing at the screen. "Connor, what's wrong?"

"Nothing's wrong. Why do you assume something's wrong whenever I call you?"

"Bad habit," I said. "Sorry."

My brother's voice softened. "Hey, I get it. I still have fucking nightmares about that phone call."

"Me too," I admitted.

"You know that Ma still apologizes to me every once in a while?" Connor said. "Eighteen years later, and she still says she's sorry. I hate it when she apologizes. Says she still feels guilty about it. As if it was her fucking fault she was too upset to call you when Dad died. She's got nothing to feel guilty about, but I can't convince her of that."

"She's Catholic," I said.

"She hasn't gone to Mass since you came out in junior high," Connor said.

"Doesn't mean the old Catholic guilt isn't alive and well within her," I said.

"Just like it is with you?" Connor said.

I didn't reply, and Connor said, "You don't have to feel guilty, you know. Ma has no regrets over leaving the church when they wouldn't support you being gay. Dad didn't either. Besides, the only reason you told them you were gay before I told them I was gay was because I was still at summer camp. If I hadn't been gone, I would have told them first and I would have been the reason they left the church."

I grunted in reply and Connor laughed. "And I wouldn't feel guilty about it either."

I glanced at my watch. "What is it you called about, Connor? I got shit to do."

"You texted me earlier and told me to call you, jackass," Connor said. "I was up to my ass in sawdust over at the Rentree job, or I would have called sooner."

"Right. Sorry." The lingering scent of Tristan's bodywash was fucking with my brain. "You finished the closet remodel yet?"

"Just about. Another few days and it'll be done. Why?"

"I have a customer who's looking for someone to build custom bookshelves for his library. Sounds like it'll be a pretty big job, the guy collects books."

"Please tell me it's that rich ass guy ... the one who also collects vintage cars."

I grinned. "It's Jack. You interested?"

"Fuck yes, I'm interested," Connor said. "Give me his number and I'll give him a call."

"I'll give him your number," I said. "Not to put any pressure on you, but if you do a good job, it'll likely lead to more work from his friends. You know how rich people are about their houses. They're always adding on shit or changing things."

"Don't I know it," Connor said. "Hey, thanks for recommending me, Shepherd. This type of work with the upper class… it could be exactly what I need to grow my business. Hell, I could maybe afford to hire an employee or two if I work enough jobs for the rich folks."

I laughed. "You're my brother, dickhead, of course I'll recommend you. Listen, Jack is a good guy, but he's not like you and me, all right? He's got more money than God and sometimes people that rich get…"

"Fucking weird," Connor said. "I get it. How weird is he on a scale of snorts blow off a naked woman's body to owns a pet lion?"

"He's not weird," I said. "In fact, he's pretty normal for how much money he has. But he's not…"

"He's not a working class stiff like the rest of us," Connor said.

"No, he definitely isn't," I said.

"I'll play it cool when I talk to him," Connor said with a laugh. "He'll never know I'm practically drooling for the job. Hey, you coming to family dinner tomorrow?"

"Yeah, why?"

"Angie's on the warpath."

"About what?"

"The florist mixed up the delivery date for the bouquets. Says she can get Angie's bouquet done, but not the bridesmaids."

"Holy shit," I said. "I didn't see anything in the news today about a florist being brutally murdered."

Connor laughed. "The florist texted her right at the end of

the day. By the time Angie got there, the store was closed. She's going over there first thing Monday though."

"Shit," I said. "Maybe one of us should go with her."

"We'll rock paper scissor that shit tomorrow night at dinner."

"We can decide like adults who will be the one to stop Angie from murdering a florist. I'm not doing that childish bullshit."

"Yes, you will," Connor said. "Hey, you fuck your employee yet? What's his name… Taylor?"

"Tristan." I glanced at the closed door, "And no, I haven't fucked him, and I never will."

"Yes, you will," Connor said with another laugh.

"You're such a dick," I said.

"Don't I know it. See you tomorrow." Connor ended the call, and I stuffed my phone back into my pocket. I leaned back in my chair and rubbed at my temples.

Connor was wrong. I couldn't and wouldn't fuck Tristan. I'd worked too hard to have my own shop and I wasn't about to ruin it by sleeping with an employee. Even if he was fucking gorgeous and pushed every single one of my buttons.

Tristan

"I can't believe you're not fired."

"Will." Ian took Will's hand and squeezed it.

"What?' Will ate a bite of pasta. "He should have been fired, and Tristan knows it."

"It's true, I do," I said to Will's boyfriend. "I'm damn lucky that Shepherd didn't fire me."

Ian poured us all some more wine. "Well, I'm glad he didn't."

"Me too," Will said. "Otherwise, Tristan would be living on my couch."

Ian laughed, and I said, "He's not joking."

"Would have made it easier to convince you to be our third," Ian said.

Will's mouth dropped open, and I couldn't help my grunt of disgust. "Gross."

"Ian, do you want a third? Because we haven't talked about that, and while I'm open to trying new things, I'm not open to it being Tristan. He's butt ugly," Will said.

"Fuck you, Will. I'm hot as hell," I said as Ian burst into laughter.

"Oh my God, I was just kidding, but it's nice to know you're so open minded." Ian leaned over and pressed a kiss against Will's mouth.

I made a gagging noise, but honestly, I really was happy for my best friend. Ian was a great guy, and while they hadn't been dating long, it was obvious that they were disgustingly in love.

I felt a pang of jealousy that I shook off. Love wasn't in the cards for me. At least not right now. I had a massive amount of debt and I was just starting a new career. Once things were a little more settled for me, then I could stop with the one-night stands and find actual love.

If it's even out there for you. It's not like you're a great fucking catch. Not with the daddy issues, and the debt, and the crush on your boss that you refuse to admit is more than just a crush.

"You okay?" Will stared at me over his glass of wine.

"I am," I said. "The pasta is really good. Thanks for having me over."

"Anytime," Will said.

Ian smiled at me. "We're glad you're here."

I knew they both meant what they said, but I wasn't stupid either. They were in a new relationship and needed their alone time. While I appreciated the weekly dinner invitation, I wouldn't intrude more than that. Not for a few more months anyway.

Ian stood and gathered the empty plates from the table. When both Will and I started to stand, Ian waved us off. "You guys sit on the deck. It'll only take me a few minutes to clean up and then I'll join you."

I followed Will out to the deck. The sun was setting, and the soft breeze kept the mosquitos at bay. We sat in the matching Adirondack chairs and Will glanced at me. "You want to talk about what happened?"

"Nah," I said. "I made a stupid mistake and got lucky that Shepherd didn't fire me. I'll be more careful next time."

"It's not like you to make that kind of mistake," Will said.

"Not according to my father."

Will made a face. "How many times do you I have to tell you that your father's a fuckwad, Tristan? You were damn good at your job in the company, despite hating every minute of it. It isn't your fault that your father is a perfectionist who sees fault in everyone but himself."

"The irony is that if I'd made this kind of mistake when I worked for Dad, he would have fired me on the spot. No second chance," I said.

"Yeah, well, like I said, total fuckwad," Will said.

We sat in silence for a few minutes before I said, "Are my father issues getting to be too much for you? Do I talk about it too fucking much?"

Will frowned at me. "Dude, you don't talk about it nearly

enough as far as I'm concerned. You need to stop bottling this shit up inside, all right?"

"You're one to talk," I said.

Will nodded. "Fair point, but if being with Ian has taught me anything, it's that you need to talk to the people who love you."

"Aw, you love me?" I said.

"Most of the time," Will said with a grin. "But you definitely need to look at doing some therapy. You might have a handle on your career now, but you're starting to make some questionable choices when it comes to your personal life. You can't just keep going home with random strangers, Tristan."

"Is this about the coke thing?" I said.

Will stared at me, his dark eyes looking right into my damn soul in the way only he could. "Yes. I didn't say anything at the time because I knew you already felt bad, but, Jesus, Tristan... cocaine?"

"I didn't do it," I said. "Hell, I didn't even have any weed that night."

"I know," Will said, "but the fact that you even contemplated trying it just because some random hookup asked you to is what worries me. That's not you, Tristan."

"I just feel... lost," I said.

"I know," Will said sympathetically. "You've had a lot of big changes in your life the last few years and you've lost the support of your family. Hell, not just lost their support, but you're guilt tripped by them all the time too."

My phone rang and I pulled it out of my pocket, staring at my mother's number as that familiar feeling of dread washed over me. "Speak of the devil."

I stuck it back in my pocket without answering it. Will gave me another sympathetic look. "Your parents are being real dickholes right now, Tristan, and the shit they're pulling on you – a therapist could help you sort it out, is all I'm saying. Okay?"

"Okay," I said.

"Oh, and also, if you even consider trying cocaine again, I will kick your ass so hard, you'll taste my boot in the back of your throat."

I laughed as Will reached over and gave me a rough side hug before kissing my temple. "I love you, man."

"I love you too."

CHAPTER 3

Tristan

I glanced at the clock on my dashboard before tapping my fingers impatiently on my steering wheel. I was going to be late if the traffic didn't clear up soon. Forced by construction to take an alternate route to work, I hadn't been prepared for the long line of traffic snaking down Wilson Avenue.

Four cars ahead, the light turned red, and our slow crawl came to a complete stop. I stared out the passenger window as I waited impatiently for the light to change. Wilson Avenue was lined with drab coloured row houses built during the fifties, and towering maple trees were in every yard. It was a low-income area, but unlike some of the other lower income sections of the city, this one was well-maintained and clean, with neatly trimmed lawns and obvious care shown to the outside of the homes.

A middle-aged man played catch with a young boy in one front yard. The little boy looked over and caught my eye. He grinned at me, revealing two missing front teeth. I smiled in return and lifted my hand in a wave. He waved back before throwing the baseball to the older man.

In the yard next to theirs, a big fluffy white dog lounged in a patch of early morning sun. He watched the traffic go by with the lazy stare of one with nothing better to do than nap. His owner came outside and sat on the front steps of her porch. The dog heaved himself to his feet and ambled over to her, resting his head on her lap. She drank her coffee and petted the dog's shaggy head before waving to an old woman walking down the street.

The old woman waved back. She had to have been in her late seventies, maybe even early eighties, I mused, as I watched her make her way slowly down the street. She wore a lime green velour pantsuit and a wide-brimmed sunhat. A plastic canary in a nest of bright green tissue paper was glued to the top of the hat. The tissue paper waved in the slight breeze.

The woman and the dog returned inside the house and I continued to watch the old woman as she walked. She held a brown cane in one hand and a large purse in the other.

I frowned when I saw the jogger headed toward the old woman. The man was staring down at his phone while he jogged and paying no attention to the sidewalk in front of him. The old woman bent down to pick something up from the ground and my alarm grew. The jogger was about to run right over her.

I buzzed down my window and shouted a warning, but it was too late. The jogger ran straight into the old woman, his thighs smacking into her head and knocking her off her feet with a thud that I almost felt more than heard.

The jogger slowed and stared at the woman lying on her back on the sidewalk before glancing around. He caught my eye and gave me a guilty grin, then took off at a dead run down the street. He turned the corner and disappeared.

"Are you fucking kidding me?" I said.

The light had turned green, and horns were honking behind me. I flicked on my signal light and pulled over to the curb. I shut off the car and jumped out, hurrying over to the woman and kneeling next to her.

"Ma'am? Ma'am, can you hear me?"

Her hat had been knocked off her head and the plastic canary in its fake green nest was sitting in the grass a few feet from her hat.

The woman stared up at me with her dark eyes. "I think so. My arm hurts though."

"Don't move," I said. I pulled my phone out of my pocket, then placed it on the ground when the old woman started to sit up. "Ma'am, I don't think you should move."

She was already in a sitting position, and I steadied her with a hand on her back as she stared at me. Her wig, a truly atrocious looking chin length bob of fake brown strands held back by a child's barrette, was off kilter, revealing the wispy fine white hair below it.

"I think my arm might be broken," she said as she cradled her left arm in her lap. "It's terribly painful. I broke my arm once before, and I remember this kind of pain."

"I'll call 9-1-1," I said. "We'll get an ambulance here to take a look at you."

"Oh, aren't you just the dearest," she said. "I'm Judith. What's your name?"

"Tristan," I said.

"It's nice to meet you. Would you do me a favour before you call 9-1-1, Tristan?"

"Sure."

"Be a dear and straighten my wig. I can feel the breeze blowing on my scalp," she said.

I straightened her wig for her, and she patted my cheek with her good hand. "My hero. There might be a handsome doctor at the hospital and I'm single. I need to look my best, don't I?"

I grinned at her. "Yes, ma'am."

She returned my grin, her bony hand sliding into mine and holding tight. "Thank you for stopping to help me, Tristan."

"You're welcome, Judith."

"YOU'RE SO GETTING FIRED," GURDEEP SAID WHEN I RAN into the shop nearly an hour late.

"I texted Shepherd and told him I would be late," I said.

"Yeah, and he's been pissed off since," Roger said. "He gave you a second chance on Saturday and you're pissing all over it already."

"I had a good reason," I said. "I'll explain and -"

"Get your ass in my office, Tristan. Now." Shepherd was standing in the doorway of his office.

I hurried into his office, closing the door behind me. "Shepherd, I can explain why I'm late. There was an -"

"What do I hate most?" Shepherd said.

I cleared my throat. "When employees are late."

"I made that perfectly clear when I hired you, didn't I? I expect you to show up to work on time every damn fucking day."

"It's the first time I've been late in six months and…"

My voice died in my throat as Shepherd gave me a look that would have cut a diamond in half. "So, you think because you've never been late before, that's a reason for being late today?"

"No, but I stopped to help -"

Shepherd's cell phone rang, and he held up his hand before answering the phone. "This isn't a good time, Angie."

He listened for a moment and alarm went through me when his big body stiffened and what looked like panic crossed his face. He gripped the edge of his desk, his knuckles white. "Where is she? Okay, I'll be there in ten."

He ended the call, and I stared at him in confusion when he pushed past me and went out the door. "Shepherd?" I trailed after him. "What's wrong?"

"Get the fuck to work," he said, "and don't be late again. Roger, I have a family emergency, you're in charge of the shop."

"Sure, boss. Everything okay?" Roger said.

"I don't know yet." Shepherd climbed onto his bike and drove out of the garage.

Shepherd

"SHEPHERD, HONEY, GO HOME. I'LL STAY WITH MOM UNTIL visiting hours are over." My mother's cool hand rested on the back of my neck.

"I'm good," I said.

"Listen to your mama," Nan said. "I'm fine. It's just a broken arm."

I visibly shuddered, and Ma's hand squeezed my neck reassuringly.

"I'm tougher than I look," Nan said.

"You shouldn't have been out walking on your own.

We've told you before that if you want to go for a walk and Ma is at work, call one of us and we'll come with you."

My grandmother was too old for a scolding from me, but I couldn't help it. The moment Angie had called me and said Nan was in the hospital, cold fear had gripped my heart. Finding out that it was just a broken arm had only eased the pressure around it a little.

She was seventy-nine years old, and while I knew she wouldn't live forever, I was nowhere near ready to say good-bye. Nan was the most important person in my life, and the thought of a world where she didn't exist made me want to bawl like a little fucking kid.

"Stop looking like I'm about to meet my maker." Nan patted my arm with her good hand. "I'm good, Shepherd. Go home and get some rest."

I just shook my head again as my mother checked her phone and my grandmother gave me an affectionate look. My siblings had left about half an hour ago, and as much as I loved them, I was glad they were gone. When the six of us got together, things got loud, and Nan needed quiet and rest.

"I told the nice young man who rescued me to come by and see me at the hospital," Nan said. "I hope he does. I gave him my full name, and the sweet girl who arrived in the ambulance told him which hospital I was going to. Do you think he'll stop by? I feel like I didn't thank him properly."

"He might," I said, although I had no real belief that he would.

I wished he would though. I wanted to say thank you. Maybe take him out for a beer, or maybe take out a loan and buy him a fucking house in some small effort to express how grateful I was to him for caring enough to stop and help a stranger.

"Tell me again exactly where you fell on Wilson Avenue," I said to Nan.

My mother laughed. "Why, so you can camp out on the sidewalk and wait for the jogger who ran Mom over to jog by again?"

"No," I said. "I'm just curious."

"Bullcrap," Mom said. "You want to find the guy and beat him up. Don't lie to your mother, Shepherd."

"How could I beat him up when Nan refuses to give me even a basic description of him?" I said.

"That's because I don't want my oldest grandson going to jail," Nan said. "Not over something like this. If you're going to prison for me, it needs to be for something cooler. Stealing me an apple red Ferrari to drive or throwing paint on those awful women who still wear real fur, now that's worth prison time."

My mom laughed again as my phone buzzed. I checked the screen and said, "Excuse me," before walking away from Nan's bed. She had a shared room, but the other patient was visiting with family in the common room. I stood on their side of the room, next to the partially drawn curtain around their bed, and answered the call. "Roger, what's up?"

"Hey, Shepherd. Everything okay?"

"Yeah," I said. "My grandmother has a broken arm, but she's all right."

"Glad to hear it," Roger said.

"Everything go okay at the shop today?"

"Yeah, no issues. Listen, Tristan said he was organizing your office after work hours. I couldn't stay late, my youngest has a gig over at Sheridan's, and I promised her I'd be there, so I gave him my key to lock up. But now, I'm starting to wonder if I didn't fuck up by trusting him to lock up the shop. He's made some mistakes the last few days and -"

"It's fine," I said.

"Yeah?" I could hear the relief in Roger's voice.

"Yes. He's made some mistakes, but he won't screw this up."

"Okay, good, good. You know, I think the kid has potential even if he…"

There was a knock on the open door of Nan's room, and I glanced up. Roger's voice faded into the background as I stared in mute surprise at Tristan standing in the doorway, holding a bouquet of yellow and white daisies. He hadn't noticed me, and I caught my breath when he smiled at my grandmother.

"Young man!" Nan's face lit up. "You came."

"Yes, ma'am." Tristan walked into the room and stood next to Nan's bed.

"Roger, I gotta go," I said in a low voice and ended the call. I shoved my phone into my pocket, staring at Tristan as he set the flowers on the table near Nan's bed and took her offered hand.

"How are you feeling, Judith?"

"I'm fine," Nan said. "Just a broken arm, like I thought."

"I'm glad it wasn't anything more serious," Tristan said.

"I'm afraid I've forgotten your name, sweetheart," Nan said.

"I'm Tristan. Tristan Mills."

"It's so lovely to see you again, Tristan. I'm thrilled that you stopped by," Nan said. Her face was beaming, and she squeezed Tristan's hand again.

"I'm sorry it's so close to the end of visiting hours," Tristan said. "I had to work a bit late tonight."

"Oh, don't you worry about that," Nan said. "Goodness, where are my manners. This is my daughter, Alison. Alison, this is the sweet young man who helped me this morning."

"Hi." Tristan held out his hand, and a smile crossed my face when my mother ignored his outstretched hand and threw her arms around him instead. My mother was a hugger and didn't, and never would, understand people who weren't.

"It is so wonderful to meet you." Mom hugged him tight, and I blinked in surprise when Tristan returned her hug without any awkwardness. "I can't tell you how grateful I am that you stopped to help Mom."

"It was no problem," Tristan said.

"Did your boss get you in trouble for being late to work?" Nan smiled at Mom. "Tristan was on his way to work when he stopped to help me."

Tristan shook his head and lied. "No, ma'am. It wasn't a problem."

"Oh good, good." Nan took Tristan's hand again and said to my mother, "Tristan is a mechanic like our Shepherd is. Oh, oh my gosh… I am just a forgetful Nancy today. Tristan, this is my grandson, Shepherd."

I walked forward as Tristan turned slowly. The look of shock on his face was almost comical. "Tristan and I know each other, Nan."

"You do?"

I stood next to Tristan and tried to ignore how fucking good he smelled. 'Yes. He works for me at the shop."

"What a small world," Ma said.

"Tristan works for you," Nan repeated.

"I'm an apprentice still," Tristan said. To his credit, he sounded almost normal, even though I could still see the shock on his face.

"Oh dear," Nan said. "That means you got in trouble when you were late this morning."

"Uh…" Tristan glanced at me. "No, I mean…"

My grandmother tutted at him before squeezing his hand.

"Don't even try to lie. We all know about Shepherd's obsession with being on time. He's been like this since he was a boy. It drives him crazy when people are tardy."

Her gaze landed on me, and although I outweighed her by a hundred pounds and was over a foot taller, I withered at her look of disapproval. "Did you shout at him, Shepherd?"

"A little." I had never lied to my grandmother and I wasn't about to start now.

"Shepherd," she said.

"It was fine," Tristan said quickly.

"Angie called before I could really start yelling," I said.

My mother laughed. "Oh, Shepherd."

"Anyway," Tristan gave me an awkward look, "I should go."

"You just got here," Nan said. "We've hardly had a chance to get to know each other."

Tristan cleared his throat. "Visiting hours are almost over and you need to rest. I'm so glad you're doing well, Judith. It was nice to meet you."

Nan caught his hand when he started to walk away. I groaned inwardly when she glanced at my mother. I knew that damn look.

"Tristan." My mother took his other hand, but to my surprise, Tristan didn't look uncomfortable or trapped. In fact, he kind of looked like he enjoyed the attention from my mother and my grandmother. "Why don't you come to family dinner this weekend? I'd love to say thank you with a home-cooked meal."

"Family dinner?" Shock returned to Tristan's face.

"Yes, you must," Nan said. "You can meet the rest of the family and we can get to know you better."

"Oh, um, I don't think, I mean that's probably…" Tristan glanced at me.

He was waiting for me to bail him out of the situation, and while I really should have, I wasn't going to. As much as I needed to keep my distance from my much too fuckable employee, what my Nan wanted, she got. I would give her the fucking moon if I could. One awkward family dinner where I had to refrain from convincing Tristan to let me fuck him in my childhood bedroom wouldn't kill me.

When it became apparent that I wasn't gonna contribute to the conversation, Tristan said, "I'm sure Shepherd would like to keep his personal and professional life separate, so…"

"Nonsense," Nan said. "Shepherd doesn't mind one bit, do you, love?"

"No, Nan," I said.

"Then it's settled," Mom said. "You'll join us Sunday night for dinner. Shepherd will give you the address. Dinner is at six, but you're welcome to come by any time after one. Family starts trickling in at all hours of the afternoon."

Tristan blinked. "Um, okay. Should I bring anything?"

"Nope, just yourself," Mom said.

With another slow look of confusion at me, Tristan turned to leave.

My grandmother refused to release his hand and pointed to her cheek. Tristan bent and pressed a kiss against her cheek, and Nan patted his face with her good hand. "You're a good boy then, Tristan. We'll see you on Sunday."

"Right, see you then," Tristan said.

Without looking at me, he left the room. I waited a beat before excusing myself and following him. He was already at the elevators and I jogged after him.

"Tristan, hey, wait a minute."

He hesitated with his hand on the elevator button. "Hey, Shepherd."

"Hey." I held out my hand, and when Tristan took it, a

goddamn fucking romantic cliché of electricity zapped through me. I dropped his hand immediately and Tristan flushed, looking uncomfortable and embarrassed.

Shit, I was fucking this up.

"I want to apologize again for being late this morning," Tristan said.

"Are you fucking kidding me? You were helping my grandmother," I said. "I'm sorry for losing my shit with you."

He just shrugged, and I said, "Thank you for helping her. Truly. Nan, she... she means a lot to me, and the thought of her lying on the sidewalk hurt and alone..."

I swallowed hard, my throat burning at just the mental image. Tristan studied me before stepping closer until our chests were nearly touching. "You okay?"

"Yeah," I said. "She just... she's special."

"I can see that." Tristan's voice had softened and lowered, and he was staring at me like I was the only person in the entire hospital. "I'm glad I was there to help her."

"Me too."

His gaze dropped to my mouth and just like that, I had a fucking hard-on.

"Saying thank you doesn't seem to be enough," I said.

"Oh yeah?" Tristan was still staring at my mouth. "What did you have in mind?"

Like it had a mind of its own, my hand cupped the back of his neck and drew him closer. I was taller than him, and Tristan let his head tilt back, his gaze locked onto mine as I lowered my mouth toward his.

His lips parted and the tip of his tongue dipped out to wet his bottom lip before disappearing into his mouth again. I wanted to follow it, wanted to taste the sweetness of him. I made a low groan when Tristan's hands gripped my hips. Fuck it, I was kissing him.

"Excuse me, are you going to block the entire access to the elevator all day?"

Tristan and I jerked apart, both of us staring at the woman standing behind us. She was pushing an older man in a wheelchair and she stared disapprovingly at us. "Is a hospital really the place to make out? There are germs everywhere."

The man grinned and reached up to pat her hand wrapped around the wheelchair handle. "Be nice, Janice. Or have you forgotten what it's like to be young and in love?"

"I'm still young," Janice said with a sniff. "But that doesn't mean I have all damn day to wait for them to stop blocking the elevator."

"Sorry," Tristan said. His face was a deep red as he stepped back so the woman could push by him. She pressed the elevator button and then watched us with bright interest.

"I should get back to Nan," I said.

Avoiding my gaze, Tristan said, "Right. Okay. Bye, Shepherd. See you tomorrow."

I nodded but stayed where I was as the elevator doors opened with a soft ding. Janice pushed the wheelchair into the elevator. Tristan followed her in, and Janice rolled her eyes at the way my gaze was glued to his ass.

Tristan waved awkwardly as the doors closed. I walked back to Nan's room, trying like hell to ignore the fact that I'd almost kissed an employee.

CHAPTER 4

Tristan

"Well, shit." I stared at the filing cabinet. I'd cleared away the piles of papers, the old car parts, and odd tools in front of it so that I could open the drawers. I had a bet with myself that the filing cabinet would be stuffed full of files, and without any clear instruction from Shepherd on what to do with the filing currently scattered all over his office, I could call it a day and go home.

Instead, the filing cabinet was completely empty. Well, not entirely empty. There were plenty of hanging file folders with blank labels, just waiting for me to fill them. I rubbed at the back of my neck and glanced at the clock on the wall. It was eight-thirty. I could go home. I'd finished my regular workday at five and been cleaning Shepherd's office since five-thirty when he'd left for the day.

But it was the first time since Tuesday that I'd worked on his office, and while Shepherd hadn't said a word to me about a timeline for having it finished, I didn't want to take months to clean and organize. I would have worked every night this week if Shepherd hadn't stayed late each night. I'd hung around until six both nights before leaving. It wasn't that I couldn't organize his office while he was in it, but after what happened at the hospital, I didn't trust myself to be that close to him.

Not when the potential for me to jump on him like a horny kangaroo was ridiculously high. Shepherd wanted me, and I had no idea what to do with that. Any other guy, I would have gone ahead and asked him out, but he was my boss. Plus, I really had no idea *why* he was into me. Roger swore up and down that Shepherd dated only twinks, and I was definitely not a twink. Hell, I wouldn't even be considered twinkish, despite what Will teasingly said.

My cell phone buzzed and I grabbed it out of my pocket, smiling a little as I answered it. "Hey, Will. I was just thinking about you."

"Oh yeah?" My best friend's voice was hard to hear over the background noise. "What are you doing right now?"

"Why?" I said.

"Ian and I are at Blackmoore's. Come join us."

Stopping at the Blackmoore Pub and having a beer and a bite to eat with Will and Ian was tempting. But my bank account was empty, and I'd be damned if I made Will pay for my beer and my meal. He was constantly buying my meals when we were out, and as much as I loved his generous nature, I hated that I was a charity case.

"Tristan? You comin' or not?" Will said.

"Thanks, but I can't," I said. "I'm working late cleaning up Shepherd's office."

"Seriously? It's almost nine on a Friday night. I think you can call it a night, bud," Will said. "You probably haven't eaten dinner, have you?"

"Not yet, but I've got some leftovers at home to heat up," I lied. "Thanks for the invite, but I'll take a raincheck."

"You sure?" Will said.

"Yeah. I really need to get this office cleaned before Shepherd changes his mind and fires me for my fuck up."

"You saved his grandma. He's not gonna fire you," Will said. "If you change your mind and want to join us, just text me, all right?"

"You bet. Bye, Will."

I shoved my phone into my pocket and stared at the piles of paper on the floor. I would start with those, sort them into a rough filing system tonight, and then check with Shepherd in the morning about how he wanted –

"What are you still doing here?"

My heart knocked against my ribs and I lurched around, staring wide-eyed at Shepherd standing in the doorway of his office.

"Holy shit." I grabbed at my chest. "You nearly gave me a heart attack. What are you doing here?"

"It's my shop." Shepherd had a large brown paper bag in one hand and his bike helmet in the other. "Why are you here?"

"Organizing," I said.

"It's almost nine." Shepherd made his way to his desk and sank into the worn leather chair behind it. He set the helmet on the floor and then opened the bag. The delicious scent of Spanish rice and grilled onions wafted out and my mouth watered. Fuck, I missed eating at the Vigilant Vegan. Will was a meat eater, and since he'd been buying my meals as of late, I deferred to where he wanted to go to eat.

"You don't have to work late on a Friday," Shepherd said.

I shrugged. "I had nothing else to do."

Could you make yourself sound like any more of a loser?

"Your boyfriend doesn't care?" Shepherd's voice was deceptively casual as he brought out a foil wrapped burrito.

"No boyfriend."

He's just making conversation, I told myself. *He's not fishing for information.*

Shepherd peeled away the top of the foil, and my stomach growled. Loudly. Embarrassingly.

Shepherd paused, staring at me over the burrito as I cleared my throat. "Uh, sorry. I'll head out. See you tomorrow."

"Tristan, wait." Shepherd's deep voice stopped me with one foot out the door.

Shepherd

What are you doing? Let Tristan leave. It's dangerous to be alone with him.

Yeah, it was. After that disastrous near kiss at the hospital, I'd avoided Tristan at the shop as much as I could this week.

Oh yeah? Then why did you come back here tonight? You knew he'd be here, especially after you made it impossible for him to stay late the rest of the week.

I ignored my inner voice and motioned to the chair on the other side of my desk. "Sit down for a minute."

Tristan glanced at the bay of the shop, like maybe he was considering making a run for it, before sitting down in the metal chair. His stomach growled again, and I reached into the bag and brought out the second burrito. I held it out to him. "Here."

His face flushed. "Oh, uh, that's okay. I have leftovers at home."

"You think I don't see the way you practically drool whenever I bring in food from the Vigilant?"

"I'm not going to eat your dinner," Tristan said, but he was eyeing the second burrito like Ma's dog, Arrow, eyed her pot roast.

"It's not my dinner. It's my lunch for tomorrow," I said.

Tristan grimaced. "That doesn't make it any better."

"Buy me one tomorrow and we'll call it even," I said.

Tristan's face did this weird twisting thing, and I knew immediately I'd said the wrong thing. Shit, how broke was the guy that he couldn't even afford to buy a burrito?

"I really should get going," he said. "Can we talk in the morning?"

"No," I said, like the bastard I was. "You're going to stay here and eat the burrito," I held my hand up when he started to protest, "without worrying about buying me one tomorrow, and we'll talk about where you're at with my office."

He continued to hesitate, and I said, "I'm not asking, Tristan."

He took the burrito and I grabbed us both a bottle of water from the mini fridge in my office. Tristan already had the foil peeled back and he bit into the burrito. The look of pure bliss on his face as he chewed and swallowed made me wonder if that was close to what his O face looked like.

My cock pressed against my jeans as if I needed any reminding of my attraction to Tristan. I peeled away the foil and took my own bite. The Vigilante's burrito was one of my favourites, and I savoured the spicy rice and their tangy house-made salsa, as Tristan ate the burrito with ravenous bites.

"God, this is good," he mumbled almost to himself.

"You vegan?" I said.

He nodded. "Yeah, for about five years now. You?"

"I've been plant based for almost fifteen years," I said. "My boxing coach got me into it. Said it would help me fight better."

"Did it?" Tristan said.

I shrugged. "It didn't make me worse."

Tristan grinned, and I studied the five o'clock shadow on his jaw for longer than I should have. What I wouldn't give to have that fine grit of stubble rubbing across my chest. I drank some water as Tristan said, "So, you do it for health reasons?"

"You don't?"

"I'm more of a no harm to animals type of vegan," Tristan said. "I mean, I want to be healthy too, but it's not my main reason for going meatless." He paused and a cute look crossed his face. "I have a cat."

"Oh yeah? What's his name?" Normally I didn't give a shit about cats, I was a dog guy through and through, but I was hungry to know every little detail about Tristan that I could. For work reasons, of course.

"Kevin."

I paused with the burrito hovering near my mouth. "Kevin? You named your cat Kevin?"

"I didn't name him Kevin, that was his name when I adopted him from the shelter."

"Yeah, but you didn't change it to something less…"

"Less what?" Tristan said.

"Less Kevin," I said.

He laughed and my cock went from a semi to fully erect. I pushed in closer to my desk and concentrated on what remained of my burrito, as Tristan said, "I wouldn't want someone to just change my name, so I didn't change his."

"Fair enough," I said.

"How's your grandmother doing?" Tristan said. "I meant to ask earlier this week, but it's been a busy week."

It hadn't been that busy, but I got the feeling that Tristan was avoiding bringing up the subject of my grandmother and the hospital as much as he could. Probably because his asshole boss hit on him.

Don't kid yourself. He was into it.

"She's good. Home from the hospital and doing well."

"Good, that's good." Tristan had finished his burrito, and he drank half the bottle of water as a flush rose up his neck. "I'm glad she's doing better."

"Me too." Awkward silence descended.

Tristan cleared his throat. "So, are we going to talk about your office?"

I looked away from his perfect mouth. "Yeah. I see you found the filing cabinet."

He laughed a bit nervously. "I did. Do you have an idea of what type of filing system you want?"

I shook my head. "Nah, not really. Probably why I never started one."

"You really haven't done any filing since you opened the shop?"

"I bought a file cabinet and hanging file folders," I said.

Tristan's laugh was more natural this time. "Did you think the papers would just magically file themselves?"

I grinned. "Something like that. Originally, I was gonna have it be part of the receptionist's duties, but it took longer than I thought it would before I could even afford to hire one. By the time I did, the filing was already out of control. I figured I'd get it sorted myself and then have them maintain it, only…"

I looked around my messy office before shrugging. I

tossed the burrito wrapper back into the bag, and held it open for Tristan to toss his into as well before chucking it into the garbage bin beneath my desk.

"Thanks again for dinner, I appreciate it." Tristan stood and walked to the filing cabinet.

Telling my cock to behave, I joined him. He smelled like car grease and whatever body wash he used, and fuck if the combination of scents wasn't the sweetest aphrodisiac.

I tried not to be too obvious about sniffing him as Tristan pointed to the biggest pile of papers. "From just moving shit around, it looks like the majority of the paperwork is a combination of work orders and receipts. I figured keeping it simple would be the best idea so, basically, I'll sort both by date and file the work orders in the top two cabinets and the receipts in the bottom two cabinets. I'd suggest just keeping last year's and the current year's in the filing cabinet. Anything from before that, can be filed in boxes by date and stored off-site."

"Sounds good," I said.

"The remaining paperwork that doesn't fall under those two categories, I'll file by type and date in the bottom cabinet. You can look through it when you have time to decide what kind of filing system you want for them. Oh, and I also had some ideas about how you could rearrange the furniture to give you some more space in your office. If you…"

I didn't mean to tune out, I really was interested in his ideas, but I loved the way Tristan looked when he was passionate about something. I'd seen it a few times before when he was talking to Roger or Gurdeep about cars, and it was just as intoxicating up close. He gestured a lot, and his face lost that pinched look of worry that always seemed to linger on him.

I knew that pinched look well. Had seen it on Ma's face

more times than I cared to remember. Hell, I'd seen it on my own face back in the early days of opening the shop. While both Ma and I were doing fine moneywise now, when you straddled the poverty line for most of your life, you never forgot what it felt like even when you were flush. It's why instead of firing him, I'd cut him a break on his fuck up with the invoicing and suggested the office organization.

Oh yeah? It had nothing to do with you thinking it would be easier to fantasize about fucking Tristan over your desk if he were actually in your office on a regular basis?

Well, yeah, there was that too.

"Shepherd? Did you hear what I said?" Tristan asked.

"No," I said. "Sorry. It's late, and I'm tired. Can we finish this talk tomorrow?"

"Oh sure, of course." Tristan looked a little embarrassed for some reason.

"Thanks."

Tristan took a few steps back and promptly tripped over the carburetor sitting on the floor behind him. As the scales of his balance tipped toward 'landing on his ass', I reached out and snagged his arm, pulling him forward.

Not expecting it, he stumbled into me. I told myself that pulling his body flush against mine was necessary to keep him upright. It had nothing to do with wanting him close.

Of course, we *were* close. His mouth was only inches from mine, those beautiful dark eyes of his filled with a mixture of surprise and... there went my dick again... lust.

It's not like I was surprised that Tristan wanted me. Even before that moment in the hospital, I'd known he was attracted to me. He wasn't great at hiding his emotions. Not that I minded. I liked knowing he wanted me. He was exactly my type, and it was getting more difficult with each passing day to ignore my lust.

I studied his mouth with an intensity that made Tristan's cheeks flush. I needed to step back, needed to let go of his arm so he could walk away. Instead, I tugged him even closer, until I could feel his chest against mine. Christ, what I wouldn't give to taste that mouth, to know what he –

Tristan's lips pressed against mine. It took roughly four seconds for me to take control of the kiss. My hand cupped the back of his neck, and I angled my mouth over his. I hoped like hell Tristan wasn't looking for sweet. I didn't do sweet. My tongue immediately demanding entrance probably clued him in.

His lips parted, and I slid my tongue inside to finally taste what I'd been aching for since the day I hired Tristan. Our tongues touched and teased, the kiss turning hot and urgent almost immediately. My hand tightened on the back of Tristan's neck when his hands gripped my hips and he leaned into me. Our lower bodies touched, and the low moan Tristan made, the way his kiss turned even more demanding when my erect cock pressed against him, sent fire through my veins.

I decided I didn't give one fuck that Tristan was my employee. I wanted him naked and on his knees in front of me with his mouth full of my dick. I pushed forward and ground my cock against him, making him stagger on his feet.

I turned him slightly and pushed him back against the filing cabinet. Tristan grunted with pain, and I froze before taking a step back.

He reached behind him and rubbed at the middle of his back. "Sorry, I just took a cabinet handle to the back."

The sound of his low voice brought back a touch of my common sense. Enough for me to realize exactly what a huge mistake I was making. As much as I wanted Tristan, I was risking everything for a fucking blow job in my office. What would Ma say if I lost my shop because an employee accused me of sexual harassment? What would Nan say?

My cock shriveled instantly at the thought, and the fire in my veins for Tristan was doused by cold, hard reality.

Tristan was reaching for me and he stared at me in puzzlement when I shook my head and dodged out of his grip.

"Shepherd? What's wrong?"

"This shouldn't have happened," I said. "Go home."

"What? No, I -"

"Go home," I snapped as I backed away until I could put my office chair between us. "Get the fuck out of my office, Tristan. Now."

With the look of a wounded puppy, Tristan left my office. I waited until I heard the bay door slam shut before sinking into my office chair. What the fuck did I just do?

CHAPTER 5

Tristan

Okay, so facing my boss after I'd sexually harassed him in his office was probably the hardest thing I'd ever done in my life, but I needed to do it. Shepherd had done a fine job of avoiding me all day. It helped that Saturday was always one of the busiest days in the shop, but it had quieted down now, and with Gurdeep and Marybeth already gone for the day, and Roger busy on the far side of the bay, this was my best and probably only chance.

I needed to apologize and hope like fuck Shepherd didn't fire me. Honestly, I was surprised I hadn't woken up to a "you're fired" text from Shepherd with instructions to clear out my shit from the shop.

You walk into his office, he's gonna fire you. You know that, right? Just keep your head down, finish your shift, and go home. You're off for the next two days, maybe that'll give Shepherd time to cool off and he won't fire you.

Doubtful.

I knocked on Shepherd's door, glancing behind me into

the bay. Roger was standing under a Chevy that was up on the third lift, opera music blaring out from his phone, and paying zero attention to what else was going on.

"Come in." Shepherd sounded pissed off, but I'd expected that. Wiping my sweaty hands on my coveralls, I opened the door and stepped inside.

Shepherd scowled at me. "What?"

"Do you have a minute?"

He stared at the screen of his laptop before nodding. "Yeah, sit down. Shut the fucking door."

I shut the door and perched on the edge of the rusted folding chair. My stomach was in knots, and beads of sweat were popping up on my forehead.

"You finish changing out the starter on the Aston?" Shepherd said.

"Yes."

"Good. Jack'll pick it up Wednesday. Make sure you check the timing before he does."

"I will."

Shepherd hadn't looked at me once since I sat down. I cleared my throat. "So, we should talk about last night."

His cheeks reddened and a muscle ticked into life in his lower jaw. I stared fascinated at it. Despite my fear that I'd be fired for sexually harassing my boss, I couldn't stop picturing myself kissing that ticking muscle.

Tristan! For fuck's sake!

The silence stretched out and my forehead got sweatier. When it became apparent that Shepherd wasn't going to respond or look at me, I forged ahead.

"I want to apologize for -"

"What happened was -"

We both stopped talking, and I cracked my knuckles nervously in the sudden silence.

"I didn't mean -"

"It can't -"

We both stopped again. The faint smile dropped from my face when Shepherd snapped, "For fuck's sake, one of us needs to go first."

"Me," I said. "I'll go first." Not that I thought apologizing and groveling for forgiveness would stop Shepherd from firing me, but it wouldn't hurt to try, right?

Shepherd made a 'get on with it' motion.

"I'm sorry about last night. I acted incredibly inappropriate, and I promise it won't happen again."

Shepherd was staring at me with a blank look of confusion on his face. I tried to plaster a "please don't fucking fire me" smile on my face but was pretty sure it just looked like I had gas.

"You're sorry," Shepherd finally said.

"Yes. Considering I'm already on probation of sorts, I know it's a lot to ask not to be fired for what happened. Still, I'm asking you to consider letting me keep my job. I'll be professional and -"

"You're fucking sorry." Shepherd acted like he hadn't heard a word of what I just said. "I come on to you, and you're apologizing for it?"

Now *my* face went slack with confusion. "Come onto... I kissed you, Shepherd. What happened last night was my fault."

"No, it was mine," he said. "I'm your boss and you felt like you had no choice." He glanced at the door to his office. "I was going to apologize to you once Roger had left."

"You were going to apologize to me?" I could hear the surprise in my voice.

Shepherd cleared his throat. "Yes. I shouldn't have used my status as your boss to force you into kissing me."

"You didn't force me into anything. I kissed you first. This is my fault."

Tristan, shut the fuck up!

"It isn't your fault," Shepherd said.

"It is."

"Fuck," Shepherd growled before slamming his big fist on top of the desk. "Are you serious right now, Tristan? I'm trying to apologize for sexually harassing you and you refuse to accept it."

"No, I refuse to accept that it was your fault when it was clearly mine," I said.

I don't know why I didn't just shut up and let Shepherd shoulder the blame. This need to keep arguing with him would only cost me my job. Still, I couldn't seem to stop. "You wouldn't have kissed me if I hadn't kissed you. I know I'm not your type and -"

"You don't know anything about me," Shepherd said. "But I'm not the type of guy to sit back and let others take the blame for my mistakes."

I flinched even though I knew what happened last night was a mistake. Still, it was fucking rough hearing the guy who gave me the best damn kiss of my life call it a mistake.

"Look," Shepherd said, "I'm sorry about last night, all right? It was a mistake, and it won't happen again. I'd appreciate it if you didn't tell the others in the shop what happened."

"I wouldn't," I said. "My personal life is my own business."

"Good." His gaze dropped briefly to my mouth before darting away. "If you would prefer not to be alone in the shop with me again, I can make arrangements to -"

Now I was the one getting irritated. "For fuck's sake,

Shepherd. I wanted to kiss you and you know it. You're not stupid, stop acting like you are."

Christ, it was like I wanted to be fired.

Shepherd's face went red, and his gaze dropped to my mouth again before he stared at a spot over my shoulder. "What happened last night was a mistake."

"Yeah, I heard you the first dozen times," I stood and stalked to the door. "Please tell your grandmother I said hello and apologize to your mother for me that I had to miss dinner tomorrow night."

"Hold the fuck up." Shepherd's low rough growl made me release my grip on the door handle and made my cock twitch. Unfortunately, it seemed that it didn't matter how pissed off I was at him, I'd never not want to fuck him.

"What?" I said without turning around.

"You're still coming to dinner tomorrow night."

I turned to face him. "That's a terrible idea."

He shrugged. "You're not fucking bailing on dinner."

"Us spending time together is a mistake," I said.

"Nan expects you to be there for dinner, and she's looking forward to it."

"So, tell her something came up and I couldn't make it," I said.

The offended look on Shepherd's face was so strong you would have thought that I'd offered to break his nan's other arm. "I have never lied to Nan, and I'm not about to fucking start now."

"Then tell her the truth," I said. "Tell her we made out in your office and now it's awkward for you because it was such a huge mistake for you to kiss me."

I sounded petulant and sulky, and I cringed inwardly but Shepherd just said, "You're coming to Ma's house for dinner tomorrow night, Tristan, even if I have to tie you up and carry you there my fucking self."

"You're being ridiculous," I said.

He glanced at the clock on his laptop. "I have work to do tonight, so I don't want you in my office organizing. Go home. I'll see you tomorrow."

"You can't just force me to go to your mother's house for dinner, Shepherd," I said.

He stood and stalked toward me, slapping both hands on the door behind me and penning me in. My cock turned to stone and my brain turned to mush. His warm breath washed over me as he leaned in until our mouths were only inches apart. "I swear to God, Tristan, if you don't show up at Ma's tomorrow night, I'll…"

"You'll what," I said as his gaze dropped to my mouth for a record breaking third time.

His nostrils flared and his blue eyes darkened with lust. "I'll strip you naked and bend you over my desk Tuesday morning."

My voice was shaky. "And then what? Spank me? I'm not looking for a Daddy, Shepherd."

He made an honest-to-god growl that lit up every one of my nerve endings. "I won't spank you. But I will spread those tight ass cheeks of yours and make you take every inch of my cock until you're fucking stuffed full of me."

"Shepherd," I breathed, "you're…"

"Every. Fucking. Inch. Tristan," Shepherd repeated.

"That's not a punishment," I said.

Shepherd's mouth twitched up in a smile. "You haven't seen how big my dick is."

"Maybe you should show me," I said.

"Maybe I should."

When he didn't move, I traced one finger down the hard

ridges of his abdomen through his t-shirt. He groaned and I breathed in the heady scent of him as he pressed a kiss against my jaw. Awareness prickled through me and I tilted my head, giving him access to kiss down my throat.

My finger was at his belt line now and I reached for the button of his jeans as Shepherd nipped my throat. His warm breath sent goosebumps popping up to life when he said, "If you undo that button, you'll be on your knees with my cock in your mouth, Tristan."

With a quick twist of my fingers, I popped open the button on his jeans.

He nipped me again before one heavy hand landed on my shoulder. He pushed, and I started to sink to my knees, jerking in surprise when there was a knock on the door.

"Shepherd? You got a minute?" Roger's voice was muffled through the door. "This transmission is being a bitch to remove, and I don't know where the fuck Tristan got off to."

I stared wide-eyed at Shepherd as he backed away and said, "I'm in a meeting with Tristan. I'll be right out."

"Oh, yeah, sure, all right."

I could hear Roger's faint whistling as he walked away.

"Shepherd," I said.

"Go," he said hoarsely. "Go home before we do something we'll both regret. Just make fucking sure you show up for dinner tomorrow night."

I wanted to argue, but Shepherd looked close to losing his cool. I yanked open the door to his office and walked out.

CHAPTER 6

Tristan

The last thing I expected when I knocked on the small and modest looking row house on Sunday afternoon, was for Shepherd to open the door holding a kid in the crook of one perfectly muscled arm.

The blue-eyed pixie of a girl stared at me from the safety of Shepherd's arms, her blonde hair in two French braids, and her mouth stained blue from the lollipop she clutched in one tiny fist.

"You have a kid," I said.

Shepherd shook his head. "No, my brother has a kid. Come on in."

I followed him into the house, taking off my jacket and hanging it on the hook that Shepherd pointed to. From somewhere in the depths of the house I could hear a TV blaring the football game, and the high-pitched laughter of a woman.

"Uncle Shepherd?" The little girl touched Shepherd's face.

"Yeah, sweetie?"

"Who's that?" She pointed her lollipop at me.

"This is Tristan. He works with me at the shop. Tristan, this is Eva."

"Hi, Eva," I said.

"You fix cars?" she said.

"I do."

"What's your favourite car?"

I blinked at her. "Uh, the Corvette Stingray LT-1. What's yours?"

"Ford Mustang Shelby GT500," Eva said without hesitating. "Corvettes are for pussies."

"Whoa… who taught you that word, Eva?" A man with dark hair and blue eyes appeared behind Shepherd. He looked so much like my boss that I knew he had to be Shepherd's brother.

"Uncle Connor," Eva said before taking another lick of her lollipop. "Him and Uncle Davey were watching football, and he told Uncle Davey that kicking a field goal inside the ten-yard line was for pussies."

The man took Eva from Shepherd's arms and kissed her cheek before smoothing back a few stray strands of her hair. "Daddy is going to have another talk with Uncle Connor about his language when there are little girls with big ears in the room."

"Your ears are bigger than mine," Eva said indignantly.

The man laughed before holding his hand out to me. "Hey, I'm Shepherd's brother, James."

"Tristan." I shook his hand. "It's nice to meet you."

"You as well. How long have you and Shepherd been dating?"

My cheeks went hot, and I avoided looking at Shepherd. "We're not dating."

"Tristan works for me at the shop," Shepherd said.

"Oh," James said. "You're the guy who helped Nan."

"Yes," I said.

"Thanks, man." James shook my hand again, his voice a little emotional as he said, "Nan is very special. You don't know what it means to us that you stopped to help her."

I nodded, feeling a little uncomfortable by the sincerity and emotion in James' voice. Before I could say anything else, a woman with dark eyes and a curvy figure joined us in the hallway. She looked to be in her early twenties, and she had a full tattoo sleeve on her right arm, a septum piercing, and pink streaks in her dark hair.

"Ma wants to know why you're making Tristan stand in the hallway instead of bringing him to the living room to join the rest of us."

"Tristan, this is my sister Nora. Nora, this is Tristan," Shepherd said.

Nora pushed past James and Shepherd and threw her arms around me. "It's good to meet you, Tristan. Nan has said a lot of good things about you. She's so special to us, and we thank God every day you were there to help her."

I made a muffled sound of surprise when Nora cupped my face and gave me a loud smacking kiss on the lips.

"Nora, take it down a notch," Shepherd said irritably.

"Oh relax," Nora said, "I'm not hitting on your boyfriend."

"He's not my boyfriend." Shepherd looked like his head might explode. "He's my employee."

"But you are gay?" Nora said to me.

"Nora!" Shepherd snapped as James made a muffled cough that sounded suspiciously like a laugh.

"What?" Nora took my hand. "It's just a question. I can't ask questions?"

"Not personal ones like that," Shepherd gritted out.

"Then how am I supposed to get to know Tristan?" Nora said. She smiled at me. "Shepherd's always so uptight. I'm straight by the way, and a Leo. You're a Taurus, right?"

"How'd you know?" I said.

Nora just shrugged. "I'm good with shit – I mean, stuff – like that." She smiled guiltily at Eva. "Sorry, baby. Auntie Nora didn't mean to say a bad word."

"That's okay," Eva said. "Uncle Connor said fuck earlier but gave me five dollars so I wouldn't tell Daddy."

She suddenly clapped her hand over her mouth and stared at James as Nora laughed and even Shepherd cracked a grin.

James sighed before kissing Eva's cheek again. "C'mon, sweetheart, let's go put the five dollars in your piggy bank."

He carried her down the hallway and up the stairs as Nora tugged on my hand. I followed her past a guest bathroom and a room with a closed door, acutely aware of the heavy foot-steps and the delicious scent of Shepherd directly behind me.

We turned right at the base of the stairs, and the hallway opened up into a combined living room and kitchen separated by a granite topped island. I blinked a little in surprise at the number of people in the small but cozy space. Shepherd's grandmother was sitting on a love seat pushed against the far wall, multiple blankets across her lap and her arm in its bright pink cast propped up with pillows. Her eyes were closed, and a soft smile was on her face.

Two dark-haired men sat on the couch in front of the tele-vision that was anchored to the wall over a gas fireplace. They were staring intently at the football game that played across the screen. A pitbull lounged at their feet, its tongue lolling out of its mouth as it grinned happily. A third man with blue eyes and prematurely thinning blond hair was sprawled in an armchair and scrolling through his phone.

A woman paced in front of him, her dark eyes flashing

fire and her long brown hair swinging back and forth like a dark curtain as she spoke into her phone. "I don't care what Jennifer said, Isabelle. The rehearsal is six pm on Friday, not six-thirty. Who's the fucking bride here? Me. I'm the fucking bride. I know when my own rehearsal is, Izzy."

She paused in front of the blond man, who blew her a kiss and patted her on the ass. She sighed and said, "The rehearsal's at six. Please don't be late. Yes, we're all going to Lavette's for dinner afterward. No, you can't bring Tony. Look, I'm sorry, but the rehearsal dinner is for the wedding party only. I'm not paying extra to feed your boyfriend when he's not even in the wedding."

She paused again before saying, "Like hell Tony doesn't eat that much. You know I love him, but the guy can eat his fucking weight in meatballs, and he weighs more than Shepherd. Don't bring him, Izzy. Swear to God if you do, he'll have to sit in the car and starve while the rest of us eat dinner. No, I'm not kidding. Yes, I will deny him fucking meatballs. No, this is not negotiable. I gotta go, doll. Yeah, I love you too. Bye."

She ended the call and plopped down into the blond man's lap. "Why didn't we just elope?"

The man grinned at her. "Are you kidding? This is your moment to shine, honey. I want everyone to see how beautiful you are and what a lucky man I am."

"Damn straight you're lucky," the woman said with a laugh before kissing his forehead.

"Tristan, I'm happy to see you again."

I turned to smile at Shepherd's mom. "Hello, Mrs. Hayes."

"Oh please, call me Alison."

I could see Shepherd wincing when she hugged me but truthfully, I didn't mind. My mother was affectionate only when it suited her, and my father had never been one to show any type of emotion toward me other than anger and disappointment.

I returned Alison's hug and smiled at her when she cupped my face. "You look good, sweetheart. Why don't you sit and visit with Mom? Shepherd will bring you a drink. Shepherd, get Tristan a drink, please."

"Yes, ma'am," Shepherd said.

"Nora, introduce Tristan to the rest of your siblings, please," Alison said before returning to the stove.

Shepherd joined her in the kitchen as Nora said, "Angie, this is Tristan. He's a Taurus. Tristan, this is Angie and her fiancé, Rob."

"Hey, Tristan," Angie said. "It's good to meet you. You're a gorgeous piece of meat, aren't you? How the hell did Shepherd convince you to date him?"

"We're not dating," Shepherd hollered from his spot by the fridge. "For Christ sake, Angie. Ma told you who Tristan was."

"Keep your panties on, Shepherd," Angie said. "I forgot. I have a lot on my mind right now. I'm getting married in seven days in case you've forgotten."

"How can we?" The older of the two men on the couch said. "You bring it up every couple of hours."

"It isn't too late to uninvite you to the wedding, Connor," Angie said.

"Empty threat," Connor said without taking his eyes from the television.

"Keep being a dickhead, and I'll sit you next to Ariel Dickenson at the reception," Angie said.

"You wouldn't." Connor's head whipped around, and he stared in horror at his sister. "She got drunk on wine coolers and kept groping me at Julie and Paul's baby shower."

"She asked me specifically if she could sit with you," Angie said. "She thinks she can save your mortal soul by – as she put it - turning you straight and back on the moral path. She's confident if you get a look at her naked bazookas, it'll zap the gay right out of you."

Connor's face turned a little green. "I really don't want to see her naked bazookas."

"Then stop pissing me off," Angie said.

Still holding my hand, Nora pulled me into the living room, stopping in front of the couch. "Tristan, this is Connor and Davey. The cutie patootie puppy-dog is Arrow."

"Nice to meet you." Connor stood and shook my hand. "Thanks for helping Nan. She means a lot to us and is very -"

"Let me guess… special," I said with a grin.

Connor returned my grin. "That's right."

I studied him for a moment. Out of all the siblings, he looked the least like Shepherd, but he was a good looking guy with his dark hair and his well-muscled body. Connor had already turned his attention back to the television, and I smiled at the second man.

He was younger than I originally thought. I'd be surprised if he was even out of his teens yet. "Hi, Davey."

"David," he said with a small scowl at Nora. "I go by David now."

"You'll always be Davey to us," Nora said as I shook his hand. She grinned at me. "Davey's the baby of the family."

Davey sighed. "I'm eighteen now, Nora. Also, you're only three years older than me. So, stop referring to me as the baby. God."

She just grinned at him before leading me over to Nan. Nora urged me to sit down next to Nan as she crouched in front of her and rested her hands lightly on Nan's knees.

"Nan? Tristan's here."

Judith's eyelids flickered open, and she smiled at Nora. "Hello, sweet girl."

"Hi, Nan. Did you enjoy your nap?"

"I did."

"Good. Tristan is here."

Nan turned her head, a smile lighting up her face. "Tristan! Hello, dearest."

"Hi, Judith. It's good to see you again," I said.

"It's so good to see you. I'm glad you joined us for dinner. I've been looking forward to it all week."

"Me too," I said as Nora stood and kissed Nan's cheek before joining Connor and Davey on the couch.

"Shepherd has as well, haven't you?" Nan said as Shepherd brought me a beer.

"Yes, Nan," Shepherd said and retreated to the kitchen.

I watched him leave, my gaze dropping to that perfect ass before I turned back to Nan. She was smiling at me in an *I know what you were looking at* kind of way. I flushed and took a swallow of beer.

"You two look so cute together," Nan said. "Why aren't you dating yet?"

My flush deepened until my cheeks felt like they were on fire. "Oh, uh, we don't... I mean, I just work for him. We're just... friends."

"You don't look at each other like you're just friends," Nan said.

I didn't know what to say and after a moment, Nan patted my knee. "I'm sorry, Tristan, I've made you uncomfortable. We can talk about other things."

She laughed when Davey made a shout of dismay, and Connor and Nora whooped and hollered and jumped up from the couch. They high-fived before Nora danced in place, gyrating her hips and waving her arms in the air, as Connor turned to Davey. "Dude, game's over. Where's my fifty bucks?"

Nana laughed again. "Tristan, honey, do you love football as much as my grandkids?"

"I think so," I said. "I used to watch it with my grandpa when I was little and now I…"

"Now you what?" Nan said.

"Now I watch it by myself."

She took my hand with her good one and squeezed. "Not anymore, dearest."

CHAPTER 7

Shepherd

I opened the back door and stepped out onto the deck off the kitchen. Tristan was leaning against the railing, staring out at the yard. Ma's raised garden beds needed weeding, and I made a mental note to stop by after work tomorrow night.

"You okay?" I stood next to him, ignoring my urge to let my hip rest against his.

"Yeah, why?" Tristan said.

"My family can be a bit… overwhelming," I said.

Tristan turned to look through the living room window behind us, and I did too. Ma and Nan were sitting sedately on the love seat, but James and Connor were having an arm-wrestling match at the island while Nora and Rob watched and, from the looks of it, Nora trash-talked them both. Davey was charging in circles around the living room, Arrow at his feet barking wildly and Eva clinging to Davey's back and laughing hysterically.

Angie marched back and forth in front of the window,

her cell at her ear. Even through the glass, it was easy to hear her. "Oh my God, Izzy. No, I don't care if Tony promises to only eat half as many fucking meatballs as usual, that motherfucker is not coming to the rehearsal dinner."

Tristan grinned and turned back to face the yard. "Your family is amazing. I like them a lot."

"They like you too," I said. "Sorry about all the wedding talk and the bickering at dinner. When all of us kids get together, we tend to fight like cats and dogs."

"You don't though, not really," Tristan said thoughtfully. "I mean, yeah, you bicker and tease, but it's obvious that it's all in good fun."

"It is," I said. Despite how fiercely I loved my siblings, I was often a little embarrassed by our collective behaviour. The only good thing about it tonight was it left very little opportunity for my mother or my nan to grill Tristan about his personal life. Nan had managed to ask him exactly two questions – did he grow up here and did he have any brothers and sisters - before my siblings had taken over the dinner talk.

"Probably makes you glad you're an only kid though, huh?" I said.

"No," Tristan said. The sadness in his voice made me move closer until our hips did touch. "I wish I had siblings. Growing up in my house could be... lonely."

"Your parents work a lot?"

He shrugged. "My dad did. My mom was a stay-at-home mom."

"Are you close with them?" I said.

He answered with a question of his own. "Is your dad not around because you and Connor are gay?"

I shook my head. "No, he didn't care that we were gay.

66

He loved us no matter what. When I was seventeen, he died in a car accident."

"Shit," Tristan turned to face me. "I'm so sorry. That must have been rough."

His sympathetic look didn't bother me the way it did when other people were sympathetic.

"It wasn't great," I said. "The worse part is that Davey doesn't remember him at all. He was only three months old when Dad died. The rest of us have at least a few memories of him, but Davey only has pictures and our stories."

"It's really awesome how your family accepts you for who you are," Tristan said.

"Yours doesn't?"

Tristan looked away. "My mother… struggles with it still, and my father is disappointed in me for a whole host of other reasons."

"They're idiots," I said.

He just shrugged. "They're not. Besides, it's no big deal. I'm an adult. I don't need their approval."

I took his arm and turned him to face me. His smile was false and so full of pain that it made my throat ache and my stomach tense. Without stopping to think about it, I wanted – no, *needed* – to comfort him. I slipped my arm around his waist and pulled him closer.

"But you want their approval," I said.

"I don't."

His nonchalant look wouldn't fool a two-year-old. I cupped the back of his neck and kneaded it gently. "It's all right if you want their approval, Tristan."

He swallowed hard, those dark eyes of his staring directly at me. "I'm never going to get it, not from either of them, so it's a waste of time and energy."

"I'm sorry," I said.

"It's no big deal," he said in a tone that made it clear it was an agonizingly big deal.

My urge to comfort Tristan, to say something – anything – to make him feel better was completely foreign to me. Feeling stupid and inept at my inability to say the perfect thing, I brushed a kiss against his mouth. "They don't deserve you in their lives if they can't see how amazing you are."

He smiled, and the combination of sweetness and desire in it made my heart knock against my ribs. "Thanks, Shepherd."

"I mean it," I said. "It's the truth, Tristan."

This time it was Tristan who pressed his mouth to mine. His hands gripped my hips, and he pulled me tight against him as he kissed me with a sweetness that made me forget entirely about my family just inside the house.

I deepened the kiss, urging Tristan to open his mouth with a sweep of my tongue across his lips. They parted, and his soft moan when I slid my tongue into his mouth made my cock stiffen.

Our tongues teased and tasted as I pushed him back against the railing. I cupped his face and stroked my thumbs along his cheekbones as we kissed. I wasn't normally tender or sweet, but Tristan and the way he kissed made me want to be sweet.

I kissed down his neck, grunting my disapproval when Tristan's hands stopped clinging to my hips and started pushing.

"Shepherd, stop."

"I don't want to," I said. "And I'm not sure you want to stop either. Not from the feel of your di-"

"Shepherd!" Tristan's voice was uncharacteristically sharp.

I lifted my head. "What's wrong?"

He jerked his chin to the left, and I glanced over to see Eva standing on the deck. I backed away from Tristan as she said, "You're kissing Tristan, Uncle Shepherd."

"Uh, I was," I said. "Do me a favour, honey, and don't tell your dad or anyone else, okay?"

She studied us for a minute before shrugging. "Okay."

"Do you promise?" I said.

"I promise."

"We should go back inside," I said without looking directly at Tristan.

I took Eva's hand and the three of us stepped into the house. Eva let go of my hand and danced her way to the island, holding her arms up to James. He picked her up and kissed her cheek. "Hi, Bunnykins. "What's new?"

"Uncle Shepherd was kissing Tristan on the deck," Eva said.

"Eva!" I could feel a stupid blush creeping up my neck as James and Connor burst into laughter, and Nora squealed with excitement.

"What?" Eva said.

"You promised you wouldn't tell," I said.

"Daddy promised I could stay up late last night, and I didn't," she said. "Shit happens."

"Eva, stop saying shit, and I did let you stay up last night," James said. "It's not my fault you fell asleep on the couch."

"What kind of kiss was it, Eva?" Nora's grin was diabolical. "Was it a French kiss?"

"Nora," Ma said.

James punched her lightly in the arm. "My kid doesn't know what French kissing is, Nora. She's five."

"Yes, I do," Eva said. "It's when you use your tongue to

lick someone else's tongue like this." She licked her own arm as Rob and Connor roared with laughter.

Eva grinned at James. "Uncle Shepherd was licking Tristan's tongue."

The blush was all the way up the roots of my hair now. Hell, I wouldn't be surprised if my fucking scalp was on fire.

"You know that's how you get cooties, right?" Eva said to me.

"Oh my God!" Connor was bent over, wheezing laughter with his face as red as mine.

"Shut it, Connor," I said.

Still laughing, he wiped the tears from his cheeks and choked out, "You should have given her five bucks to keep quiet. That's what I did."

"It didn't work," Nora said. "Eva told us you said fu – the eff word in front of her."

"Eva!" Connor stared at her in disbelief. "That five bucks was to buy your silence."

Eva just giggled. I turned to Tristan, worried that he was embarrassed or humiliated, but he grinned at me immediately, his cheeks only a little red.

"Sorry," I muttered under my breath.

"It's no big deal," he said as Angie stopped in front of us.

She stared at me and then at Tristan. "You're coming to my wedding."

"Um, I'm sorry?" Tristan said.

"You," Angie poked him in the chest, "are coming to the wedding and the reception and dance this Saturday."

"Oh, uh, I work Saturdays," Tristan said.

"Lucky for you, I'm your boss's favourite sister so -"

"Hey!" Nora said.

Angie ignored her. "So, when I tell him to give you the day off, he's gonna do it."

"I really appreciate the offer but -"

"Do you have a suit?" Angie said. "Because if you don't, you're about Rob's brother's size, and you can borrow his. He's in the wedding party, so he's wearing a tux."

"I have a suit," Tristan said. He looked off-balance and confused, which was often the case for people when my sister Angie was around. She was a force of nature and denying her what she wanted only made her more determined.

"Fantastic. I'll get your number from Shepherd and text you the details."

Tristan glanced at me. "I'm sure it's too late to add extra people for the dinner and -"

"It's a buffet, there's plenty," Angie said. "I won't take no for an answer, Tristan. Tell him, Shepherd."

I realized with a jolt that I wanted Tristan to come to Angie's wedding. I wanted it very much, in fact, but from the look on Tristan's face, it was the last thing he wanted. Swallowing my disappointment, I said, "Angie, you can't just order people to go to your wedding. Tristan doesn't want to go."

"No, it's not that," Tristan said quickly.

"See?" Angie said triumphantly. "He wants to go."

"Angie, he's not -"

"Shepherd, hush, dearest," Nan said.

I closed my mouth with a snap as Nan joined us. She took Tristan's hand and squeezed it. "Honey, obviously, if you don't want to go to Angie's wedding, you don't have to. But it would mean the world to me if you did."

She glanced at me, a small smile crossing her face. "And to Shepherd. Isn't that right, sweetheart?"

"Yes, ma'am," I said.

"Well, if you're sure..." Tristan said hesitantly.

"Positive," Angie said. "We want you there, don't we,

babe?" She glanced at Rob, who nodded and gave the thumbs up.

"The more the merrier, man."

"Then we're good." Angie walked away as Tristan stared up at me.

Nan squeezed his hand again. "I'm so happy, sweet boy. I have a new dress and a new wig for the wedding, and Nora says they make me look like I'm sixty again. I'll probably need you to beat the single men off me with a stick."

My breath caught in my throat when Tristan smiled at Nan. "I look forward to it, Judith."

Nan returned his smile. "Call me Nan."

CHAPTER 8

Tristan

I knew immediately that the man standing in reception was Jack Walker. Owner of more classic cars than I could count, and, according to Roger, the richest man in town. I didn't doubt Roger's claim in the least. Not when the man wore a thousand dollar suit and a five thousand dollar watch.

I wiped my hands again, even though I'd already cleaned them, and held out my right. "Mr. Walker? I'm Tristan Mills."

Jack shook my hand, his grip dry and firm. "You've been working on my cars the last few months."

"That's right," I said.

"Shepherd's said a lot of good things about you," Jack said.

I hid my pleased expression. "Shepherd's out of the shop at the moment, but I'm happy to go over your work order with you and explain what I did to the Aston."

"Sure," Jack said.

Marybeth joined us, smiling up at Jack. "Are you sure I can't get you a cup of coffee or glass of water, Mr. Walker?"

"I'm sure. Thank you, Marybeth."

"You're welcome. If you change your mind, just let me know." She gave him a cute and flirty smile before returning to the reception desk, making sure to put plenty of sway in her hips.

Jack watched her go with a bemused smile on his face before glancing at his watch. "Ready when you are, Tristan."

"Sure. I know Shepherd usually shows you what we did, but if you're pressed for time, I can just verbally go over the information and -"

"I have time," Jack said. His hazel-coloured eyes studied me intently. "Lead the way, Tristan."

I led him through the bay to his car. I popped the hood and pointed out what I had done, and while he listened closely and nodded in all the right places, there was more than once that his gaze drifted down my body.

When I was finished talking, Jack nodded and held out his hand. "Looks great. Thanks for all your hard work, Tristan, not just on the Aston but on my other cars as well."

"My pleasure." I wasn't surprised when Jack's grip lingered in mine. "It's good to finally meet you in person."

"You as well." Jack dropped my hand, his gaze falling on my mouth for the barest of seconds before he smiled at me. "Would you like to have dinner with me, Tristan?"

I couldn't help my smile. "How did you know I was gay?"

Jack shrugged, leaning against the car and crossing his arms across his wide chest. "I'm very perceptive about people's sexual preferences."

My grin widened and Jack returned my smile. He was an attractive man with broad shoulders and narrow hips, and the perfectly tailored suit highlighted his ass and thick thighs nicely. His light brown hair was on the short side, and I was

74

sure if I stepped close enough, I would see flecks of green in his hazel eyes.

He was definitely my physical type, and he was interested in me. So why did I have zero attraction to him? I tried to tell myself that it was because he was a client and Shepherd would disapprove if I dated a client, but I couldn't quite convince myself that was the only reason.

"What do you say, Tristan?" Jack said. He straightened and stepped closer. So close I could confirm that yes, he did have pretty flecks of green in his eyes. "Dinner tonight? I know a great pasta place over in Millwoods. Say around seven?"

"Oh, uh -"

"Tristan's working late tonight." Shepherd's gruff voice made me twitch. I took a step away from Jack, the back of my legs bumping into the front fender of the Aston as I smiled guiltily at Shepherd.

"Hey, Shepherd. I was just going over the Aston with Mr. Walker."

Shepherd didn't quite step between me and Jack, but his big body blocked a good portion of mine as he stared coolly at Jack. "Hello, Jack. Thought you weren't coming by until later."

"My appointment ended early. It's good to see you, Shepherd." Jack held out his hand and after a moment, Shepherd shook it grudgingly.

"Come into my office and I'll go over the invoice with you," Shepherd said.

"No need," Jack replied. "Everything looks good."

"Great." Shepherd held his hand out in my direction, and I placed the clipboard with the work order and the keys to the Aston in his hand. "I'll walk you to reception."

"Sure. But before we go," Jack stepped around Shepherd, "are you free tomorrow night, Tristan?"

"He's working late all this week," Shepherd nearly growled.

"The weekend then," Jack said with a smile at me. "I'm busy Saturday, but free on Sunday."

"Sunday doesn't work for him," Shepherd said.

Jack glanced his way, raising an eyebrow. "Do you always answer for your employees, Shepherd?"

"When our biggest client is hitting on them at their place of fucking work, and they think they're obligated to say yes just to keep their job, yeah, I fucking answer for them," Shepherd said.

A scowl crossed Jack's face. "Tristan is not required to go out with me in order for me to continue giving the shop my business. Frankly, it's insulting that you're insinuating I conduct my personal life in such a manner."

Shepherd's face reddened. "Maybe if you didn't hit on my damn -"

"Hey," I said and stepped in front of Shepherd. "Everything's cool." I scooped the clipboard from Shepherd's hand. "Shepherd, Roger was looking for you. Why don't you talk to him, and I'll get Mr. Walker squared away at reception?"

Shepherd was still staring at Jack like he was two seconds away from banning his best customer from the shop. I turned my back to Jack and stared directly at Shepherd, placing my hand on his abdomen and rubbing lightly. "Roger's looking for you."

He blinked and looked away from Jack, studying me for a few seconds before turning and walking away. I took a deep breath and turned to face Jack. "Let's head back to reception."

BY THE TIME I'D FINISHED PULLING THE ASTON AROUND
front and saying goodbye to Jack, Shepherd was in his office
and Gurdeep and Roger were both staring at me like I'd
grown two heads.

"What?" I said.

"I heard Jack asking you out. You gonna go out with him
or what?" Gurdeep rubbed at a smear of grease on his arm.

"No," I said.

"Why not? The dude's loaded," Gurdeep said.

"I had no idea he was gay, did you?" Roger said.

"No, I've never met the guy before," I said. "Also, it's
rude to listen in on private conversations."

Gurdeep shrugged. "Some guy's gonna shoot his shot like
that, I'm gonna watch. Maybe I can get some tips, you
know?"

Roger laughed. "You still haven't worked up the courage
to ask Angelina out?"

"Nah, not yet."

"Time's a wastin, my friend, and you're not getting any
younger," Roger said before slapping Gurdeep on the back.
"Fortune favours the brave and all that shit."

"Tristan!" Shepherd's voice echoed across the bay. "My
office. Now." He stomped back into his office and slammed
the door shut.

Roger stared mournfully at me. "How many times have I
told you that pissin' in Shepherd's cornflakes is gonna get
you fired. What did you do this time?"

"Nothing," I said. "He's just in a bad mood."

"You'd better get your ass in there before he really does
fire you," Roger said.

I crossed the bay to Shepherd's office, knocked on the

door, and let myself in without waiting for his answer. He was pacing back and forth in the clear space I'd made in front of his desk like an angry bull.

I shut the door and studied him calmly. "What can I do for you, Shepherd?"

"Did you tell that asshole Walker you would go out with him?"

"How is that any of your business?" I said.

It was the wrong thing to say. Shepherd's scowl deepened, and he stalked across the office until we were only inches apart. "You're not going out with him."

"Since when did you get to dictate how I conduct my personal life?" I was playing a dangerous game, but there was a small part of me that wondered just how far I could push Shepherd into kissing me. Call it childish, but I was enjoying Shepherd's obvious jealousy.

"He's our biggest customer," Shepherd said.

"I'm aware," I said.

"I don't want you dating him."

"It's not up to you." I said. "Was that all you wanted to tell me, or was there something work related?"

"This is work related," Shepherd ground out. "Dating our biggest customer is not allowed."

"Show me where it says that in the employee handbook," I said with a grin.

"Tristan," he said warningly.

"What?" My smile turned innocent. "Jack's a good looking guy, and it's been a while since I've had my dick sucked. Maybe -"

Shepherd made a sexy growl that sent tingles down my spine before pushing me up against the door and kissing me hard. I rubbed my body against his as we kissed, the feel of our cocks brushing against each other tore a moan from my throat.

Shepherd pulled back slightly, his breath coming hard and fast as he stared at me. "He is not sucking your dick, Tristan."

I grinned, my lips still tingling from the bruising pressure of Shepherd's mouth against mine. "Yeah, you're right. He strikes me as the type who'll have me on my knees and sucking *his* dick. Which, you know, I'm totally willing to... fuck! Shepherd!"

His name escaped my mouth in a soft little moan. His hand rubbing my dick felt amazing, and when he gave me a little squeeze through my coveralls, I nearly embarrassed myself by cumming right there.

"The only dick your hot mouth will be sucking is mine," he growled into my ear as his hand rubbed and caressed.

"Promises, promises," I moaned.

He muttered a curse, and I would have been pissed that he moved his hand from my dick if he wasn't unbuttoning his jeans and pulling down the zipper. He shoved his jeans down his thighs, dragging his briefs with them. I swallowed hard when I saw his dick. It was ridiculously long and thick, and my mouth watered when a drop of precum spilled from the slit.

Shepherd's hands were already on my shoulders, and when he pushed, I dropped to my knees immediately. One hand wound in my hair and pulled tight while the other gripped the base of his magnificent cock.

"Open," he demanded hoarsely.

I opened and moaned with sheer delight when Shepherd pushed his cock deep into my mouth. He groaned, his hips thrusting forward and his hand tightening in my hair.

"Fuck, Tristan," he breathed when I sucked hard on his

dick before cleaning away the precum from the tip. "Oh fuuu-uck, that's so good, baby."

I bobbed my head along his dick, sucking and licking at his cock like a man possessed. Shepherd groaned again before his hand tugged painfully on my hair and made me hold still.

"Keep your mouth open for me and your eyes on my face," he growled.

I stared obediently up at him as he fucked my face. He wasn't sweet or gentle, but his roughness was an unbelievable turn on. I couldn't help but rub my cock through my coveralls as he used my mouth. He breathed my name again, his hand cupping the back of my head as he thrust deep into my mouth. I tried to breathe through my nose, tried not to gag as the head of his cock brushed the back of my throat.

"Fuck," Shepherd grunted softly. "I wanna cum in your mouth."

I pushed him back enough to say, "do it," before sliding my lips over his thick length again.

"Oh fuck," Shepherd said, "you sure, baby?"

I nodded, and he brushed his thumb along my cheek in a rare moment of sweetness before his hand gripped my hair again and he fucked my mouth with fast and furious strokes. I only had a sharp inhale of breath, a slight stiffening of Shepherd's body as a warning before his hot cum filled my mouth.

He tasted incredible and I swallowed every delicious drop as I stared up at him. His hot gaze never left mine, and he made another low groan when I finished by licking the head of his cock clean. He twitched and jerked and sucked in harsh pants of air as he pulled me to my feet.

He kissed me hard, his tongue invading my mouth, his hand reaching down to grip my dick. "Your turn," he whispered against my mouth.

He reached for the zipper of my coveralls, both of us freezing when there was a knock on the door leading into the reception area.

"Shepherd?" Marybeth said. "Do you have a minute to talk to Mrs. Gareth? She's stopped in because her car is making a weird knocking sound, and she's insisting only you can look at it."

Shepherd's jaw clenched and he pressed his forehead against mine. "Be right out, Marybeth."

"Okay, thanks."

Shepherd inhaled deeply before stepping back and pulling up his pants. He stared at me, and I could see the exact moment that the pleasure faded, and regret took its place. "Tristan, I shouldn't – I mean, that wasn't…"

"Wasn't what?" I said as my cock went limp, and my giddy excitement deflated.

"That wasn't appropriate, and I apologize."

I cringed at the formal and guilty tone of his voice. The look he was giving me made me feel ashamed. "Don't," I said. "Don't look at me like that. I wanted this to happen."

"It shouldn't have happened."

"But it did," I said.

"Yeah." He buttoned and zipped his jeans before shoving his hand through his hair in a frustrated gesture. "This was… you were… a mistake. It won't happen again."

"A mistake," I echoed.

"Yes. I'm sorry."

"Stop fucking apologizing," I said. I couldn't stand to hear him call me a mistake, not when the taste of his cum was still in my mouth.

"I have to talk to Mrs. Gareth," Shepherd said.

"Yeah," I said. "I need to get back to my work. My boss can be a real asshole sometimes."

It was a stupid and pointless thing to say, but my feelings were hurt, and my emotions were a rancid stew, and I couldn't be in Shepherd's office another fucking minute. Not with the look of regret and shame on his face.

I turned and yanked open the door, leaving Shepherd's office without another word.

CHAPTER 9

Shepherd

"Dude, you don't look so good," Davey said solemnly.

I avoided pulling on the stupid bowtie around my neck even though it was way too tight and I could hardly breathe. But it had taken Nora forty-five minutes to get it right, and she was close to tears by the time she finally finished. Telling her it was too tight would have sent her over the edge.

Not that I could blame her. I was feeling a little *over the edge* myself, and for once, it had nothing to do with Tristan and what happened in my office a few days ago.

I twisted my neck from side to side, hoping it would help loosen the bowtie before grunting out, "I'm fine."

"You sure?" Davey said. "Because you look like you might pass out or throw up."

"Or both," James said.

I scowled at them as Connor rested a hand on my shoulder. "You'll be fine, Shepherd. It's just a two minute walk down the aisle. No one will be looking at you anyway, right? They'll all be staring at Angie."

"Yeah, I know," I said, but even just Connor mentioning what I was about to do in less than – I glanced at my watch and fresh sweat beaded up on my forehead – half an hour made my chest tighten and my heart thud.

"Maybe you should walk her down the aisle," I said to Connor.

Connor gave me a sympathetic look but shook his head. "Angie wants it to be you, buddy. I know this is hard for you, but it's important to her, right?"

I swallowed hard. "Yeah."

We were in some tiny room in the back of the church waiting for the rest of the wedding guests to arrive. It wasn't warm in the room, but I could feel my shirt sticking to my back with sweat, and the air felt thick and liquid-like.

Davey elbowed James. "I don't get why he's got stage fright over this. It isn't like in high school when he had to do that speech in front of the whole school and he fainted."

"Please stop bringing that up," I gritted out. "It's not helping, Davey."

"No one will be looking at you," Davey said.

"I heard Connor the first time." My stomach rolled and churned.

"Hey, did you see Tristan?" James said. "He looks great in his suit."

I knew he was only trying to help, trying to distract me from my upcoming task, but it wasn't helping. I'd been miserable all week at work, and it wasn't because Tristan was pissed at me. He should have been, hell, I *wanted* him to be, but he wasn't. He was… indifferent. He spoke to me when required, and to anyone who didn't know him better, it even looked like he was his normal, friendly self.

But I knew the real Tristan now, and the warmth that had disappeared from his gaze when he looked at me, the way his voice never held that note of softness anymore when we spoke, had me tied up in knots and full of shame at what I'd done to him.

He told you he wanted it to happen.

Yeah, he did, and while I knew he wasn't lying, the fact that I'd stuck my dick in my employee's mouth in my own damn office made me a real fucking asshole.

"Shepherd?" James touched my arm. "Did you see Tristan?"

"No." Bile rose in my throat. I pushed my way past James and toward the door.

"Where are you going?" James called.

"I need some fresh air," I croaked. "I'll be right back."

Without waiting for their reply, I left the room, stumbled my way down the hallway, and practically ran out the back door of the church. I made my way across the parking lot to the small, wooded area to the right of the church.

The number of cars in the parking lot made my anxiety crank up another notch – Christ, why did Angie invite so many damn people? - and the bowtie around my neck seemed to tighten. Gasping, I leaned against the solid trunk of an oak tree and pulled at the bowtie, trying to loosen some of the pressure without actually untying it.

My heart was racing and sweat was pouring down my face and the tightness in my chest was turning unbearable. I could barely breathe, and a buzzing sound had started in my ears. I was becoming lightheaded, and I wanted to sink to my knees before I just fell over, but Angie would kill me if I got dirt on the tux.

"Shepherd? Hey, you okay?"

Tristan's voice washed over me like a soothing balm. I

raised my head and, not caring what it looked like, I grabbed for his hand. My head buzzed and my breath tore in and out of my chest in ragged gasps. "Can't... breathe."

Tristan pressed me back against the tree, the trunk solid against my back as his hands reached for my bowtie. I tried to swat his hands away, but he said, "Hold still, Shepherd," in a sharp tone I'd never heard before.

I let my hands drop as Tristan untied the bowtie and unbuttoned the first few buttons of my shirt. "You're having a panic attack and you're hyperventilating." He pulled a handkerchief from his pocket and wiped the sweat from my face. "You need to slow your breathing down."

"Can't," I gasped, "not enough air. Can't..."

"You can," he said firmly. "Like this." He took a deep breath in through his nose and blew it out his mouth. "Breathe with me, Shepherd."

He pressed his forehead against mine and gripped my hips, holding me tight. I tried my best to mimic his breathing.

"Concentrate, honey," Tristan murmured. "Deep breath in through your nose."

I breathed in through my nose with him, exhaling out my mouth when he did.

"Good, honey," Tristan said. "Again."

I don't know how long we stood there, our foreheads pressed together and our breaths mingling as we took breath after breath, but when Tristan finally pulled back a little, the tightness in my chest was gone, and I no longer felt like my heart might simply explode.

"Better?" Tristan said.

I nodded. "Yes. I'm sorry."

"You don't have to apologize for a panic attack," he said.

"No, I'm sorry about what happened in my office, about —"

"Stop." Tristan's voice lost its sweetness, and I could have kicked myself. "Please don't keep apologizing. I'm told I'm a mistake enough from my father, I can't bear to hear it from you too."

I stared at him in shock. "Tristan, I don't think you're a mistake."

"You called me a mistake in your office," he said.

"No, I... that wasn't what I meant. I meant what we did – what *I* did – was a mistake. I took advantage of you, used my power as your boss to -"

"Bullshit," Tristan said. "Knock it off with the martyr act, Shepherd. I wanted what happened to happen just as much as you did, and it's insulting for you to pretend I didn't."

I took another shaky breath. "Shit. I just keep fucking this up, don't I?"

"You really do," Tristan said.

His blunt honesty made me smile and relief swept through me when Tristan smiled in return. "How do you feel?"

"Still a little shaky," I said. I wasn't feeling shaky anymore, but I didn't want to lose Tristan's hold on me. Not yet. Not after I'd been craving it for the last three days. "How did you know I was out here?"

"I was at my car grabbing some mints," he said. "I saw you stagger across the parking lot."

"Thanks for checking on me. I wouldn't blame you if you'd just left me to vomit and pass out."

He frowned, his hands tightening a little on my hips. "I wouldn't do that, Shepherd. I care about you. A lot."

I swallowed hard as warmth flooded my stomach, banishing the last of my nausea. "I care about you too."

His smile sent my heart into overdrive again, but this time in a good way.

"Why are you having a panic attack?" he said.

"Stage fright," I said. "I'm walking Angie down the aisle and just thinking about all those people looking at me…"

"They won't be looking at you," Tristan wiped the sweat from my forehead with his handkerchief, "they'll be looking at your sister."

"I know, it's just…"

"What?" he said.

"When I was in high school, my English teacher had us submit essays to a local contest. My essay won first place. I was given a medal and five hundred bucks, and I had to make a thank you speech in front of the entire school. I was nervous, but I didn't know how nervous until…"

"Until what?" Tristan said.

"Until I went to do my fucking speech and fainted," I said. "I smacked my head on the floor so hard, I had a concussion and needed ten stitches."

I waited for him to laugh like most people did when they heard the story of a man who looked like me being so fucking scared, he fainted. To my surprise, Tristan cupped my face and ran his thumb over my cheek. "I'm sorry that happened to you. It must have been terrible."

I nodded, my throat too tight to speak.

"But," Tristan squeezed my jaw, "that's not going to happen today. Today, you're going to walk your sister down the aisle while everyone stares at her, not you, and give her away."

"What if I can't do it?" I said. "What if I freeze up and can't walk her down the aisle? Anytime I've tried to do anything in front of a large group of people, I… I panic and freeze and make a fool of myself. This day is so important to Angie, and with Dad gone, it's up to me to make it perfect. What if I fuck it up?"

"That isn't going to happen," Tristan said. His thumb

caressed my cheek again. "You can do this, honey. I know you can."

"You really believe that, don't you?" I said.

"Yes."

"A kiss would probably help convince me," I said.

He laughed and leaned in to press a kiss against my lips. When I tried to deepen it, he pulled back. Tristan must have seen the disappointment on my face because he smiled and said, "Trust me, I would love nothing more than a heavy make out session with you, but now is not the time. I know I don't know Angie all that well, but I'm pretty sure she'd murder me if I made you late for her wedding."

"Yeah, she really would," I said. "She's tougher than me."

Tristan laughed before kissing my forehead. "The wedding starts in ten minutes. You ready to walk Angie down the aisle like a boss?"

"Yes, but the wedding's gonna be delayed. It took Nora forty-five minutes to tie this bowtie. She might kill us both when she sees it's undone."

Tristan grinned and buttoned my shirt before reaching for the ends of the tie. "I got you, boo."

To my astonishment, he tied the bowtie in less than three minutes. He smoothed it and then patted my chest. "How's that feel?"

"Good," I said. "Not nearly as tight… I may not choke to death after all."

He took my hand. "Let's go."

"How'd you know how to tie this?" I pointed to the bowtie as we headed across the parking lot.

"My dad taught me when I was a teenager." His voice didn't change, but his body stiffened at just the mention of his father. I wanted to talk to him about his dad, wanted to know the name of the guy who made Tristan feel so low, but now was not the time.

We were nearing the door of the church and I slowed down a little as I looked Tristan up and down. He wore a dark charcoal coloured suit with a light blue tie and shiny black dress shoes. The suit fit him perfectly, almost like it'd been tailored for him. Now that my panic attack had passed, I could appreciate just how fucking good he looked. I would never have suspected that Tristan would look so comfortable in a suit, not after wearing oil-stained coveralls five days a week.

"That suit fits you great," I said.

He laughed and I felt like an idiot. I wasn't used to complimenting the guys I wanted to fuck. It wasn't my style. Either they wanted to fuck me, or they didn't, and I wasn't putting in the extra effort to change their mind. There were plenty of other options out there.

Only, it was different with Tristan. I wanted him to know how good he looked, wanted him to know how hot I thought he was. Too bad I fucking sucked at giving compliments.

"I mean," I cleared my throat, "that suit looks really expensive. Shit."

Tristan laughed again, and I tried a third time. "You look really handsome, Tristan."

"Thank you. You look very handsome as well." He squeezed my hand. "You ready?"

"I think so." I took a deep breath and then leaned in and kissed Tristan. "Thank you."

"You're welcome, Shepherd."

CHAPTER 10

Tristan

"So, why are you the only one in your family who doesn't dance?" I sat down at the table across from Shepherd and reached for his beer. He let me have it without protest, and I took a large swallow and handed it back.

"Two left feet," he said. "I'm a terrible dancer."

"Is that the truth or do you just hate to dance?" I fanned my hand in front of my face, trying to cool myself down. I'd lost the suit jacket a while ago and rolled up the sleeves of my dress shirt, but after nearly two hours of dancing, I had sweated through my shirt, and I could practically see the steam rising from my face.

"It's the truth." Nora collapsed in the chair next to Shepherd. Her face was flushed, and her feet were bare, and she was just as sweaty as I was. "He's a horrible dancer. Why do you think Connor danced with Mom and Nan instead of Shepherd? Neither of them wanted bruised feet from when he stepped on them."

Shepherd poked her in the arm. "We can't all be ballet dancers like you."

"You're a ballet dancer?" I said. "That's cool."

"I was," Nora said. "Until I started to hit puberty. Us Hayes ladies are known for our glorious tits and asses. My ballet instructor wanted me to starve myself, but I decided I enjoyed eating more than ballet, so I quit and took hip hop instead. Thanks to this guy."

She put her arm around Shepherd's shoulders and kissed his cheek affectionately. "If it hadn't been for him, I wouldn't have had dance lessons, and Davey wouldn't have played football or soccer."

"What do you mean?" I said.

"Nothing," Shepherd said quickly. "She's just drunk and when she drinks, she gets… mushy about shit."

"One, I am not drunk," Nora said. She hiccoughed and then giggled. "Well, mostly not drunk, and two, I don't need to be drunk to be mushy. Besides, why shouldn't Tristan know what a great guy you are? If you want him to date you, you gotta sell the whole package, not just wear tight jeans so he can check out your ass."

She grinned at me. "The Hayes boys are also known for their asses."

I laughed as Shepherd rolled his eyes. "Go join Davey and James on the dance floor, Nora."

"In a minute." She rested her elbows on the table and smiled at me. "My brother is the best, Tristan. After Dad died, things were tough money-wise. He had a life insurance policy, but it was small and only covered the hospital bills and funeral costs. At that time, Mom wasn't even back to work yet cause Davey was only three months old. She went back to work a few weeks after Dad died, and Nan looked after Davey, but workin' as a secretary doesn't exactly cover the costs of raising six kids, you know?"

I nodded as Nora turned a hero-worship gaze to Shepherd. "Shepherd was seventeen when Daddy died. He had a part-time job at Walmart on the weekends, but he talked to his boss and convinced him to put him on the night shift full time. He worked from eleven to seven five nights a week unloading trucks and stocking shelves, while he did his last year of high school. He'd come home from school, do his homework, sleep for a few hours and then go to work. I don't know how he did it without, like, dying of exhaustion. Every bit of money he made from his job went straight to Mom to help with bills and shit. He got top marks in school too, enough to win a couple of grants that paid for him to take the auto tech program over at Woodwise College."

"Wow," I said. "That's really impressive."

"Okay, Nora," Shepherd said, "enough story-telling for one night."

"Not done the story yet, big brother," Nora said with a grin. "So, while Shepherd was taking the auto tech program, he met this dude who owned a boxing gym. The guy suggested he give boxing a try. Turns out, Shepherd was pretty good at it, and the gym owner convinced him to start training with Austin."

"Who's Austin?" I said.

"This super good boxer from back in the day. He didn't box anymore, but he trained a bunch of guys. When he saw what a natural Shepherd was, he said he would train him and get him booked in for some fights. Said it was a good way to make some quick cash if Shepherd could take a punch and stay on his feet."

Her face lost some of its cheeriness. "Mom and Nan

didn't want him to do it. They were worried about him getting hurt, but technically he was an adult and they couldn't stop him." She glanced at Shepherd. "It's the first and only time Shepherd's ever gone against Nana's wishes."

I studied Shepherd in the dim light of the reception hall. He gave me an embarrassed smile, and I wondered if he had any idea how incredibly amazing I thought he was.

"Anyway," Nora took Shepherd's hand and squeezed it, "Shepherd kicked ass at boxing and won a lot of fights, and his prize money went to us younger kids. It paid for all the extras we never would have had otherwise. Me and Davey, hell, Angie too, had amazing childhoods because of him."

She leaned in and kissed his forehead. "We won't ever forget it either, big brother."

I could see tears in Nora's eyes. My own eyes were stinging, and my throat was tight, and even Shepherd's eyes were rimmed with red. He squeezed Nora's hand but didn't say anything as Eva, her white flower girl dress stained with something very large and very red, skipped over to us.

"Auntie Nora, come dance with me!" She climbed into Nora's lap and patted her face. "Daddy's tapping out."

Nora laughed and kissed Eva's cheek. "You can't blame him, honey. He's old, remember?"

"Really old," Eva said solemnly.

"What did you get all over your dress?" Nora said before touching the stain. "Wait, is that wine?"

"Yep," Eva said with a laugh. "Uncle Connor spilled it on me. Daddy called him a dink and then Uncle Connor called Daddy a dinkless dink, and then Auntie Angie came over and said they were both dinks, and if they didn't stop fucking swearing in front of me, she'd kick them both in the jewels."

I pressed my lips together to stop from laughing as Shepherd made a muffled snorting sound.

"I didn't even know Daddy and Uncle Connor had jewels," Eva said as she touched the diamond hoop in Nora's septum. "They never wear them like you do, Auntie."

Both Shepherd and I burst into laughter. Eva stared curiously at us as Nora laughed and stood up, holding Eva on one hip. "C'mon Eva-girl, let's dance."

She headed for the dance floor. Shepherd took a drink of his beer before handing it to me. I finished off the last swallow and said, "Your family is amazing."

"They are," Shepherd said. "Insane, but amazing."

'You're the oldest, right?"

"Yeah. Connor's a couple years younger than me, then James, Angie, Nora, and Davey."

"Do Eva and James live with your mom?" I asked.

Shepherd nodded. "He and Eva's mom had their own place, but when she took off last year, James needed help with Eva. He works full time, and Eva didn't start kindergarten until this year. So, he moved back in with Ma and Nan, and between the three of them, Eva had someone to watch her while James was at work."

"Does Eva see her mom at all?"

"No. She worked as a bartender over on the south side and met some crazy rich dude from California who was here for work. Two weeks later, she left James and Eva and moved to California with the guy."

"You're kidding me," I said. "She just left her kid?"

"The rich guy didn't like kids, said they weren't part of his life plan, so Torrie left Eva with James. She used to video chat with Eva once a week the first couple of months, but James said they haven't heard from her at all in nearly eight months. He's called her a bunch of times so that Eva could talk to her, but she never answers. About a month ago, the number was no longer in service."

"What a shitty thing to do to your kid," I said.

Shepherd shrugged. "Eva's better off with James anyway. Torrie never really cared for being a mom."

"Do you want kids?" I said.

"Yeah. You?"

"At least two," I said.

We sat in silence for a few minutes as the music blared and the guests danced. It was close to midnight, but the party was still going strong. I had a feeling that the Hayes clan would party well into the night.

"You did really great walking Angie down the aisle," I said.

Shepherd grimaced. "I felt like everyone could tell I was about two minutes away from vomiting or passing out."

"You looked a little nervous but nothing crazy," I said. "I'm proud of you."

He hesitated and then took my hand. "Thanks for your help. I wouldn't have been able to do it if it hadn't been for you."

"I don't believe that," I said. "You're strong, Shepherd. The shit you've been through…"

He shrugged. "Plenty of people had it worse than me."

"Maybe," I said, "but that doesn't mean your struggles aren't valid."

He studied me for a moment and then said, "Will you tell me why your dad thinks you're a mistake?"

"I will, but not tonight," I said. "Tonight is about love and family and celebration."

I thought he might argue, but instead, he said, "Will you come home with me tonight, Tristan?"

"Yes," I said. "I will."

"I LIKE YOUR PLACE," I SAID.

"Thanks." Shepherd had given me a quick tour before leading me back to the kitchen. It was a bungalow with three bedrooms and a small backyard. Compared to the shitty one-bedroom apartment that I could barely afford, Shepherd's house seemed like a mansion to me.

"You want a beer?" Shepherd said.

I shook my head. What I wanted was to have a quick shower and then lie on my back in Shepherd's king-sized bed while he fucked me into the best orgasm of my life. But things felt a little strange and awkward between us now that it was just the two of us in his house.

"You okay?" Shepherd was studying me in the bright light of the kitchen.

"Yeah. You?"

"If you've changed your mind, that's fine."

"I haven't," I said. "Have you?"

"No, but it feels…"

"Awkward. Weird," I said.

He grinned. "Yeah."

He crossed the few steps of the kitchen to join me and pulled me up against him. "Do you have any idea how much I want to fuck you, Tristan?"

"Roger told me about a week after I started that you only dated twinks," I said.

Shepherd snorted. "Look, for a middle-age straight guy, Roger tries hard to understand our," he made quotation motions with his fingers, "culture, but the guy thinks a twink is any gay guy who doesn't have tattoos."

I laughed hard. "Roger's really great. So is Gurdeep."

"They are," Shepherd said. "I'm lucky to have such competent guys working at the shop." He pressed a kiss against my mouth. "You included."

"Yeah, especially when I missed billing my own fucking time," I said.

He shrugged. "Mistakes happen. Don't doubt yourself, Tristan. You're good at what you do. Really good. If I didn't think you were, I wouldn't let you work on Jack's cars."

"I honestly thought you hated me," I said as I put my arms around his shoulders.

"I was a dick because I convinced myself if you hated me, it would be easier to ignore how much I wanted you," Shepherd said.

"Well, it didn't work. I never hated you," I said. "I was too busy wondering how you'd sound when you were buried in my ass."

His nostrils flared, and he squeezed my ass. "Why don't we go to my bedroom and you can find out."

"I was sweating a lot at the reception," I said. "Do you think I could have a quick shower first?"

"Only if you let me join you so I can wash your back," Shepherd said.

"Deal." I followed him to his bedroom, and we shed our clothes. I smiled a little at the careful way Shepherd hung the tux and placed it in his closet.

"It's a rental," he said before walking to the adjoining bathroom. He turned the shower on, and as the water heated, he pulled me up against him again and kissed me slowly. "I didn't expect you to look so fucking hot in that suit. You wear it like you've worn a suit your entire life."

I just shrugged, not wanting to explain my past life when I was so close to finally getting what I'd wanted from the day I started working at Shepherd's garage. The bathroom was getting steamy, and Shepherd opened the glass door of the shower and stepped inside. I joined him, laughing a little at the tight fit with both of our big bodies.

"What?" Shepherd said as he urged me past him so I was under the spray of hot water.

"I was picturing some serious sexy time in the shower," I said as I dipped my head under the water, "but I was also picturing a bigger shower."

Shepherd grinned as he soaped his body before handing the soap to me. "I should have taken you to the guest bathroom, it's a tub/shower combo and bigger."

"Next time," I said, then could have kicked myself. For all I knew, Shepherd would kick me out of his house as soon as the fucking was over.

Shepherd leaned forward and pressed a kiss against my wet shoulder. "You're not great at hiding your emotions, so, just FYI, you're staying the entire night with me."

I relaxed a little. "Is that right?"

"Yes." Shepherd reached down with a palmful of soap and gripped my fully hard dick. He cleaned it with slow strokes as I leaned back against the slick shower wall and tried not to embarrass myself by cumming right there and then.

"I guess I could do that," I gasped out when Shepherd made a twisting motion with his wrist that started a fire burning through my veins.

"Good." Shepherd let go of my dick, ignoring my moan of protest, and pushed me under the hot spray of water. "Rinse off so I can get you in my bed."

I couldn't even come up with a smart-ass reply. I just rinsed quickly, my dick throbbing with need, and then switched spots with Shepherd so he could rinse away the soap. We were out of the shower, toweled dry, and in his bed less than five minutes later.

Shepherd opened the nightstand drawer and brought out a condom and a bottle of lube. He set them next to the lamp before lying on his side and running a finger up and down my stomach. "You okay with leaving the light on?"

"Hell yes," I said. "I'm not giving up the chance to see your body."

His laugh turned into a low moan when I turned to face him and our erect cocks brushed against each other. I reached down and wrapped my hand around both of us, rubbing slowly as we kissed. I sucked on his tongue as he cupped my ass and squeezed it.

"Fuck, I love your ass," he said. He circled a finger around my anus, studying my face. "How do you feel about rimming?"

"Love giving and receiving," I said. "You?"

"Same."

"This is an excellent start for us," I said.

Shepherd laughed. "So far, so good."

"Are you an, *I do the fucking only* kind of guy or…?" I raised an eyebrow at him.

He shrugged, his finger still circling my asshole and lighting up all the sensitive nerve endings. "I usually top, but I can switch it up if you like to top."

"Usually a bottom," I said. "But also willing to switch things up."

I let my head fall back, my hand still gripping us tight when Shepherd kissed my neck. He trailed a path of hot kisses across the sensitive skin before nipping at my earlobe. "You were driving me crazy shaking that ass of yours on the dance floor at the reception."

"Oh yeah?" I let go of my dick and concentrated solely on Shepherd's, circling my thumb over the tip before rubbing his shaft from the base to the tip.

"Hmmm," he groaned and sucked on my lobe, sending

shivers racing up and down my spine. "I kept picturing how that ass would look in my bed with my cock deep inside of it."

I huffed out a breath when his finger probed lightly at my hole. "Maybe we should find out."

"Soon," he said before kissing across my chest.

I cried out when his firm lips brushed across my nipple. He sucked it into his mouth, laving it with his tongue as I clutched at his head with one hand and rubbed his dick with the other. "Please, Shepherd!"

"Begging already?" he said with a small grin before sucking on my other nipple.

His hot mouth felt crazy good, and I rubbed my dick against his abdomen, smearing a glistening path of precum across him.

That hot mouth was currently working its way across my stomach and I flipped to my back, pushing on the top of Shepherd's head, urging him lower. His low laugh warmed me, and I ran my hand through his dark hair before tugging lightly. He glanced at me, and I said, "Suck me, Shepherd."

"Soon," he said before he went back to investigating every inch of my abdomen with his tongue. When he circled my navel and then bit at my hip bones, I arched up, my cock brushing against his hard chest.

"Fuck!" I said. "Shepherd, I need your goddamn mouth."

"So impatient," he said, but his hot mouth settled over my aching cock, setting off a thousand fireworks in my brain.

I cried out, my body bucking helplessly against the pressure of his sucking mouth. His fingers pressed against my taint, massaging my prostate and making me writhe and moan. He cupped my balls and played gently with them before returning to my taint. He pressed hard, his hot mouth taking me down to the base as he hollowed his cheeks and sucked.

I shouted his name, my hips arching as I came hard into his mouth. He swallowed all of me, cleaning off my cock with his tongue as I moaned and twitched and quivered.

"Fuck, I'm sorry," I gasped out as Shepherd rose to his knees and rolled the condom onto his cock. He coated his dick with lube before pushing on my knees.

"Why are you sorry? Open for me, baby."

I spread my legs wide, my body still twitching as Shepherd coated my hole and two of his fingers with lube then slid his fingers into me. I clenched around him, and he groaned before scissoring his fingers and stretching me a little.

"Didn't warn you," I gasped out. "Should have said something, but it..." I sucked in another gasp of much needed oxygen, "took me by surprise."

"I don't mind," he said. "You taste fucking delicious."

"Thank you," I moaned as his fingers stretched me in the most satisfying of ways.

He laughed. "You're welcome, baby. Are you ready for me?"

"Fuck, yes," I said.

He knelt between my legs, pushing them up until my knees were almost at my chest. I hooked my hands under my knees and held my legs up as Shepherd pressed his cock against my hole.

He stared at me as he pushed in. When my eyelids started to drift close, he squeezed my thighs. "No, Tristan. Look at me as I'm making you mine."

A soft thrill went through me at his words, and I stared directly at him as he entered me inch by inch. I blew my breath out, trying to relax as he rubbed my thighs.

"Good," he praised softly. "Push back against me."

I pushed against the pressure, grunting when he slid in a few more inches.

"Fuuuck," he muttered in a low, drawn-out groan. "You're like a fucking vice around my dick."

"You're welcome," I panted.

He huffed out a laugh as he sank fully into me. We hadn't broken eye contact once, and while it should have felt weird and intense, it didn't. It felt... perfect.

"You're beautiful," Shepherd said, his hand reaching to caress my chest.

My throat tightened, and my voice was hoarse when I said, "So are you."

He gripped my legs and made a few long and slow thrusts. "Good?"

"Yes," I said. "You can go harder, honey."

He groaned and immediately gave me two hard and quick pumps that rocked my body and made me tighten around him.

"Oh fuck," he said with a genuine sound of panic that made me grin. "I'm gonna cum."

"That's the idea," I said before rocking against him.

"Not this quickly," he gritted out. "I got a fucking reputation to protect."

My grin turned into a laugh, and his moan turned into a muttered curse before he fucked me with hard thrusts, his hands tightening around my thighs as the teasing look on his face was replaced with cold, hard need that made my stomach tighten with anticipation.

"You still good?" he said.

"Yes. Fuck me the way you want to," I said. "The way you need to."

My name on his lips sounded like a prayer as he pounded

into me, his hips working back and forth like a piston as he found his pleasure in my body. He didn't last long, but considering I didn't last even three minutes with my dick in his mouth, I wasn't about to judge. Besides, there was something intoxicating about watching him lose control so quickly, watching what my body did to him.

He breathed my name, his head falling back and the cords in his neck standing out in harsh ropes as his body shuddered then stilled and he drove deep one final time. His hands clamped on my thighs and his hips bucked as he emptied his load into my ass.

I rubbed his chest and his abdomen, watching his face as he moaned quietly before collapsing on top of me. I rubbed his back as he buried his face in my throat.

After only a few minutes, he heaved himself up, supporting himself on his hands as he stared down at me. "Holy fuck."

"Yes," I said. "The holiest."

He stared blankly at me then burst into laughter. I grinned up at him and kissed his jaw. "You mind getting off me? All those rippling muscles are heavy as shit."

He slid out of me and disposed of the condom in the attached bathroom before returning to the bed and climbing in beside me. "You want to be the big spoon or little spoon?"

I hid my surprise that he even wanted to spoon. "Little," I said and turned on my side.

Shepherd pressed up against my body, wrapping his arm around me and kissing the back of my shoulder. "Thank you, Tristan. That was crazy good."

"It was," I said. "Let's do it again."

I was joking, but Shepherd kissed my shoulder again and said, "Give me twenty minutes."

I laughed. "I appreciate the enthusiasm but considering

that it's," I craned my head to stare at the alarm clock on the nightstand, "almost three thirty in the morning, maybe we can sleep for a few hours and fuck later?"

Shepherd yawned. "Deal. Night, Tristan."

"Night, Shepherd."

CHAPTER 11

Shepherd

"You don't have to make me breakfast." Tristan sat at the small island in my kitchen, watching as I poured the blueberry and oat mixture into the waffle iron.

"I want to," I said. "Besides, my blueberry oat waffles are award winning."

"Award winning, huh?" Tristan's smile was contagious. "Well, now I have to try them."

"You definitely do." I closed the waffle iron and then set a cup of coffee in front of Tristan. "I have almond milk in the fridge if you need it."

"Just black for me." He sipped at the coffee. "What are your plans for today?"

"There's the gift opening at Angie and Rob's place at two," I said. "How about you?"

"Thinking I might go to the garage and work on your office. I'd like to get the filing done by the end of the day. With all the paper filed, I can start organizing the other stuff this week and maybe have it done completely by Friday."

I leaned against the counter. "You don't have to finish the office thing. It doesn't -"

"Don't," Tristan said. "Don't do that, Shepherd."

"Don't do what?"

"Don't change the rules at the shop just because we fucked last night. I screwed up and cost you a lot of money. You've cut me a break by giving me the chance to make up for it instead of firing me. I want to do this, and I don't appreciate you going soft on me about the fuck up because you like how it feels to be in my ass."

"All right." I kept my voice mild and my body language casual. Tristan was normally easy-going, so for him to get this riled up this quickly, meant I had fucked up with him.

"Is this it for us?" Tristan said abruptly.

I gave myself some time to answer by putting Tristan's waffles on a plate, adding more blueberries on top of the waffles, and setting the plate in front of him with the maple syrup. "Do you want it to be?"

"You know I don't, but..."

My stomach dropped. "But what?"

"I'm not sure I want to be known as the guy who fucks his boss," Tristan said. "And I know for a fact that you don't want Roger or Gurdeep, or hell, the customers, knowing you're fucking an employee."

I hated that he was right, but it was true. I'd always kept my personal life and my work life separate for a reason. "We could keep it on the down-low."

"I don't want to be someone's dirty little secret, do you?" Tristan said.

"No."

"Besides, if we got into a fight or broke up, work would be awkward as fuck. And I need this job."

"I know you do," I said. "For the record, I wouldn't fire you if we did fight or stopped dating."

"I know, but it would make it tough on both of us to be at work." He cut a piece of waffle and popped it into his mouth. "This is good."

My appetite had completely abandoned me, and from the look on Tristan's face, his had too. He was just being polite. I sank into the chair across from him, picking at a chip in the top of the table. Tristan not thinking I was worth the risk was a sharp knife to the gut, but I understood it. I'd been where he'd been, knew what it was like to constantly worry about finances, and I would do the same thing if I was in his shoes. The need to eat, to have a roof over your head, was more important than dating someone.

So, why did I want to plead with him to give me a chance?

"I wish it were different." Tristan poked at his waffles. "Maybe when I'm done my apprenticeship… it's only another two years."

"Yeah, maybe," I said.

Tristan pushed his barely touched waffles away. "I'll do some asking around town. There might be another shop looking to hire an apprentice."

I appreciated the effort he was making, but knew it was pointless. There were exactly two other mechanics who were willing to hire an apprentice in this town, and neither of them were hiring. We both knew it. If Tristan wanted to find another job at a garage, he'd have to drive three hours round trip every day to the closest city, Riverton.

"I should go." Tristan stood up and I did too, reaching across the table to snag his hand.

"You don't have to leave yet. The gift opening isn't for another few hours."

He smiled at me but pulled his hand free. "I know, but I'd like to get started on the office."

I wanted to argue that he would have time to work on my office even if he stayed a little longer with me, but what good would it do? A relationship with Tristan wasn't possible and both of us knew it.

"ARE YOU FUCKING KIDDING ME, GURDEEP?" I GLARED AT him before picking up the wrench he'd left on the hood of Jack's 1957 Ford Thunderbird. "You don't leave your fucking tools – tools that can scratch a forty-five hundred dollar paint job - on the hood of the fucking car. Are you trying to lose me my best client, is that it?"

"Sorry, Shepherd." Gurdeep took the wrench from me. "It won't happen again."

"Make sure it fucking doesn't," I snarled before stalking away.

"Shepherd?"

"What?" I scowled at Marybeth as she stepped into the bay, regret washing over me when her face fell. I'd been a real shithead all week to everyone in the shop, and if I didn't rein in my emotions, I would lose some excellent employees. I needed to do what Tristan was doing – keep my head down and my mouth shut and do my fucking job.

I scrubbed my hand through my hair, not even caring that I was getting grease in it, "Sorry, Marybeth. What's up?"

"Mrs. Gareth is here again. Her car is acting up, she says."

I held in my sigh of exasperation with the effort of a man lifting a tank. It was close to quitting time on Friday. After five days of not having Tristan in my bed, of missing his touch and the way his voice lowered and went delightfully hoarse when I touched him, I was in no mood to search for Mrs. Gareth's non-existent car trouble while she hovered and tried to convince me to date her granddaughter.

"Should I tell her you're busy and to come back tomorrow?" Marybeth said timidly.

"No. I'll talk to her." Pasting a smile on my face, I walked toward reception.

BY THE TIME I'D LOOKED OVER MRS. GARETH'S CAR, listened to her extol the virtues of her granddaughter, and weaseled my way out of yet another coffee date invitation with said granddaughter, nearly forty-five minutes had passed, and the garage was empty. I didn't give a shit that Roger and Gurdeep had left without saying goodbye, but I wished I could have seen Tristan once more before he left.

Which was ridiculous because I'd see him right here at work tomorrow morning, but as of late, I was incredibly ridiculous when it came to anything Tristan related. I stopped in reception where Marybeth was shutting off the computer and turning the phones to voicemail.

"Have a good night, Shepherd. I'll see you tomorrow," Marybeth said as she headed for the door.

"You too." I locked the door behind me, thankful that Marybeth didn't seem to be holding a grudge toward me for my asshole behaviour. I'd have to apologize to Gurdeep and Roger tomorrow, which I wasn't fucking looking forward to. Apologies didn't come easy for me.

If you'd kept your dick to yourself instead of fucking Tristan, you wouldn't be in such a foul mood.

I ignored my inner voice. Not that it wasn't right, but I

didn't need a constant reminder that as amazing as being with Tristan was, it was also the biggest mistake of my life. I had no fucking idea how difficult it would be not to fuck him again.

I stepped into my office from the reception side. My mouth went dry, and my dick went hard as I stared at Tristan's delectable ass bent over my desk. He wasn't wearing his coveralls and his jeans clung to that perfect ass, the one that I'd dreamed about nightly. My favourite fantasy of fucking Tristan over my desk flamed to life right in front of me.

Like a man in a dream, I moved closer as Tristan muttered a curse and stretched even further over my desk to grab for a piece of paper that was floating off the edge.

I shouldn't do this - couldn't do this - but it didn't stop my hands from gripping Tristan's hips, didn't stop me from pressing my dick against his ass and grinding hard.

Tristan jumped in surprise, making an adorable gasp that turned into a moan when I ground my dick against him again.

"Are you purposely trying to get me to fuck you against my desk, Tristan?"

He craned his head to look over his shoulder. "No, I was doing the last of the organization of your office. I'll be finished tonight if…"

"If what?" I reached under him and popped the button on his jeans before pulling down the zipper.

"If I don't have any interrup… oh fuck, that feels so good." Tristan arched into my hand as I reached inside of his briefs, took his dick into my hand, and pumped him firmly.

I used my free hand to yank his t-shirt up around his shoulder blades so I could kiss his lower back. "You know what I think?"

"What's that?" Tristan panted as his dick grew thick and hard in my hand.

"I think you waited until you heard me in the hallway, then bent this perfect ass of yours over my desk because you want me to fuck you."

"I... hmm... I can't think when you do that," Tristan moaned.

I kissed his back again. "I'm going to fuck you, Tristan. If you don't want me to fuck you, now's the time to say so."

He made a cute zipping motion across his lips with his fingers, and I grinned at him. "Lose the shirt."

He pulled his shirt over his head and shoved his jeans and briefs down to his ankles. I pulled a condom from my wallet and opened the drawer in my desk as Tristan said, "We need lube."

"I've got it covered," I said.

He grinned at me over his shoulder. "You'd better not be about to use some axle grease on my ass. Because as much as I want to fuck you right now, I'm pretty sure that stuff isn't recommended for fucking."

I smoothed my hand over his ass as I rummaged in the drawer. "Relax, baby. I've got some lube somewhere... here it is."

I pulled out the travel size bottle of lube as Tristan laughed. "Do I even want to know why you have lube in your office drawer?"

"Probably not," I said before bending down and biting Tristan's ass cheek.

He jerked and hissed in a breath. "Shit, maybe try not to leave bite marks."

I soothed my bite with a soft lick, enjoying the sound of his quiet moan. "Sorry, baby."

I pulled my shirt over my head and pushed my jeans and briefs down to the top of my boots. I rolled the condom onto my dick and then slicked it with lube. "Spread your cheeks for me."

Tristan reached back and spread his ass cheeks. I poured lube on his tight hole, massaging it in before adding more and slowly pushing two fingers into his ass. He hissed out another breath, pushing back against me with a soft groan. "God, that feels good. I need your cock, Shepherd."

"Soon," I said as I changed the angle of my fingers and brushed against his prostate.

He cried out, his body arching up off my desk. I reached around him and took his dick in my hand again, rubbing with long slow strokes as Tristan's breath turned harsh and fast.

He pumped his hips into my hand, his ass gripping my fingers as he braced his hands on the desk for support.

"You look so fucking hot," I said. "Do you have any idea how many times I fantasized about fucking you over my desk, baby?"

"Then do it. Christ, I'm dying over here," Tristan groaned.

I laughed and tightened my grip on his cock, jacking him with harder strokes as he panted and cursed and moaned. "Shepherd, please!"

"Did you imagine this?" I said as I released his cock and pulled my fingers free of his tight ass. I spread his cheeks and lined the head of my cock against his hole. "Did you picture me fucking you over my desk, Tristan?"

"Daily," he moaned. "Shepherd, stop talking and fuck me already!"

I pushed, both of us groaning when I slid smoothly into Tristan. I pushed again, watching as Tristan took my dick to the base. "Oh fuck," I muttered. "You feel so good, baby."

"You too," Tristan panted as he rocked back and forth on my dick. I held his hips loosely and let him control the pace, trying not to blow my load right away as Tristan squeezed hard around me.

"Keep doing that and I won't last," I said.

"That's the idea," Tristan said as he reached under him and gripped his own cock. He stroked himself with quick and hard movements as I started to meet each rock of his hips. "Oh God, yes, like that, Shepherd."

I leaned over and pressed a kiss against his back before fucking him hard and rough. He met each of my thrusts with reckless enthusiasm. The feel of his tight ass, the sounds of his low moans and groans pushed me closer and closer. I increased the pace, fucking him so hard that the desk scraped across the floor.

Tristan planted his feet and jacked himself hard and fast as the sound of our bodies slapping together echoed in my office. With a harsh cry, Tristan arched and came, his ass squeezing my dick, his hand jerking his cock as his cum landed in splashes across the surface of my desk.

I bellowed his name, my hands clamping down on his hips as I thrust deep and came in a rush of pleasure. I rocked against Tristan, my body shaking, before I pulled him into a standing position and wrapped one hard arm around his chest. He turned his head and we kissed, our tongues tangling together as we came down from the high of our orgasms.

I released his mouth and buried my face in his neck, inhaling his scent as he rubbed his hand along my arm.

"I got cum on your desk," Tristan finally said.

I laughed and raised my head, staring at the top of my desk. "At least the desk wasn't covered in work orders. Thanks to you."

He grinned at me, and I pressed a kiss against his mouth before easing out of him. I disposed of the condom and pulled up my pants as Tristan pulled up his jeans and buttoned them.

"I'll get some paper towel and disinfectant to clean off your desk," he said.

I caught his hand before he could leave my office. "Tristan, will you come home with me tonight?"

He hesitated, and the happiness and content I felt for the first time since he left my house on Sunday faded. "Forget it. I shouldn't have asked you to -"

"It's not that." He leaned forward and pressed a kiss against my collarbone. "It's Kevin."

"Your cat," I said.

He nodded. "I feel bad leaving him alone all day and all night. But," his look was uncertain, "if you wanted to come home with me..."

"Yes," I said. "Fuck, yes."

CHAPTER 12

Tristan

"Kevin hates me."

"Kevin doesn't hate you."

"He clawed my ass while I was fucking you, Tristan. There was blood."

"And crying."

Shepherd glared at me before rolling over and pushing the sheet down so I could stare at his magnificent ass and the lines of scratches that covered one perfect cheek. "My ass looks like Wolverine took a liking to me, and you're gonna call me out for a few tears? Besides, it wasn't crying, it was... intense eye watering."

I laughed so hard that Kevin jumped off the end of the bed and strolled out of the room.

"I'll take that apology any time now," Shepherd called after him before lying on his back. The sheet had dipped low on his flat abdomen and I leaned over and nuzzled the neatly trimmed patch of pubic hair. He groaned, his hand coming down to cup the back of my head.

I kissed below his navel, my fingers stroking Shepherd's abs as the sheet tented. My own cock was hard and dripping even though Shepherd had just given me the best blow job of my life not even an hour ago.

I kissed his stomach. "You're really good at sucking cock."

"Thank you." He grinned at me, his hand stroking through my hair as I rested my chin on his stomach and stared up at him.

"You need to stop staring at me like you want to fuck me when we're at the garage," I said.

"I do want to fuck you."

I laughed. "Okay, but if you think Roger and Gurdeep aren't going to notice the way you look at me, you're wrong."

"Maybe you shouldn't bend over the cars so much and show off your ass," Shepherd said.

"It's literally my job to bend over cars."

Shepherd ran his thumb over my bottom lip. "Yeah, it is, and you look fucking hot doing it."

I laughed again but then said, "I'm trying to be serious here, Shepherd."

He studied me silently, his hand still petting my hair. Shepherd had come home with me Friday night and, to my surprise, spent the night with me. He'd left early Saturday morning to grab a fresh change of clothes before going to work. He'd been in a fantastic mood Saturday at the shop. After his moodiness of the last week, I knew it was a welcome relief for Roger and Gurdeep.

I'd lingered after closing, taking my time cleaning up my tools as Roger and Gurdeep and Marybeth left one-by-one. I didn't have any real belief that Shepherd would want to fuck again, but both me and my dick were willing to wait around to see. I'd nearly fallen over but had been quick to say yes when Shepherd offered to pick up dinner from the Vigilant Vegan and bring it back to my place.

"I really like fucking you, Tristan," Shepherd finally said.

"But..."

"But nothing. That's it. I really like fucking you." Shepherd tucked his other arm under his head.

"I like fucking you too, but we both agreed that it wasn't a good idea."

"What if I've changed my mind?" Shepherd said.

"You want to be my dirty little secret?" I said.

"I want to be your dirty everything," Shepherd said with a grin.

I smiled and sat up, stroking my hand across his stomach. "What if it doesn't work out? What if you find me annoying after only a few months and dump me?"

"That's not going to happen."

"You don't know that," I said. "You don't know me well enough to know if I'll be annoying or not."

"Give me the chance to find out," he said before sitting up. "I promise things won't be awkward at work, all right? Even if it doesn't work out between us, I know how to keep things professional. Give *us* a chance, Tristan." He rubbed my thigh through the sheet.

"There is a lot of stuff about you that I really want to learn more about," I said.

"Oh yeah?" He grinned at me, his hand moving to rub my inner thigh. "Like what?"

"Like how a big, tattooed, motorcycle riding ex-boxer, could be so cuddly."

Shepherd's hand stilled on my thigh, an uncertain look crossing his face. "You don't like it?"

I pushed him onto his back and straddled his hips. "I love

it. It's just unexpected. You don't look like the cuddling type."

He rubbed my bare thighs, his cock hardening under my ass. "Does that mean you're willing to give us a chance?"

"Yes," I said. "If you're okay with not announcing it at work for a while. I think we should give it at least a month or two before we decide when or if we make it obvious at work that we're dating."

He nodded. "Yeah, okay. His thumbs massaged the crease between my thighs and my pelvis, a smile crossing his face as he watched the way my dick hardened. "You're so fucking sexy, Tristan."

"So are you." I leaned down and we kissed, our tongues brushing in long, slow strokes as Shepherd squeezed and kneaded my ass.

"I want to ride you," I said.

"Be my guest, cowboy." Shepherd's grin made me laugh. I reached for a condom and the lube, wiggling back so that Shepherd could roll the condom on while I massaged lube in and around my hole before lubing Shepherd's dick.

He moaned, his hips rising with the grip of my hand. "That feels good."

"This will feel better." I lined myself up with his thick cock, using one hand on his chest to balance as I gripped the base of his dick with the other hand and lowered myself down. His cock felt amazing and we both moaned quietly as I eased my body down until he was fully sheathed.

"Fuck," Shepherd breathed as I settled on top of him, "I can't get over how fucking tight you are."

I braced my hands on his chest and rode him with slow strokes. Shepherd tucked both hands under his head and kept his big body still, letting me take control as he stared unblinkingly at my face. I kept up the same slow pace, smiling as

Shepherd's breathing slowly changed and his hips began to rock. I loved watching him lose control, loved watching the way my body could drive him crazy.

I reached down and stroked my dick, rubbing my thumb over the head as Shepherd groaned and his hands reached for my ass. He held me steady and thrust upward, going a little deeper and making me gasp.

"Okay?" he asked, his body stilling under me.

"Yes," I said. "Don't stop."

He moved again, our bodies rocking against each other, our breathing growing louder and faster as we both reached for our orgasms. I kept my gaze trained on his face, memorizing every perfect part of it as he smiled up at me.

When his big hand wrapped around my dick and rubbed firmly, I gasped, and my ass tightened around his dick.

"Fuck!" He made short and hard thrusts that I rode with pleasure as his hand jacked me harder.

"Oh fuck," Shepherd moaned, his back arching before he drove deep. "Oh God, I'm gonna cum... I'm gonna..."

His voice trailed off in a long moan and his body hitched for breath as he came in my ass. I knocked his hand away and rubbed my dick, crying out when my own orgasm washed over me. We both shook with the intensity of our orgasms, and I gripped his hips with my knees to keep my balance as my frantic grip on my dick slowed.

I slumped forward, resting my forehead on Shepherd's chest as his breath stirred my hair. He stroked my sides and my hips. "That was amazing."

"Hmm," I agreed before easing off of him and lying on my side next to him.

Shepherd took off the condom and tossed it in the trash can beside the bed before putting his arm around me. I reached for the towel I'd tossed carelessly at the bottom of the bed after my shower and cleaned off my cum from Shepherd's stomach and my own. When I was finished, I dropped the towel on the floor and laid beside him. I rested my cheek on his chest, listening to the heavy beat of his heart.

"How's your butt?" I said.

He laughed. "How's *your* butt?"

I sat up. "Fine. But I want to know if the great cat scratching tragedy of early Sunday morning means the only sex position you'll be willing to participate in from now on is me riding you."

"Would that be so bad?" he said with a grin.

"Variety is the spice of life," I said as my stomach growled.

Shepherd kissed my forehead. "Let's shower and go for a bite to eat."

My bank account wouldn't let me eat out, but I didn't want to admit that to Shepherd. "Why don't we stay in and I'll make us something to eat?"

"You don't have that much food in your house," Shepherd said.

My face heated. "I'll get some groceries this week."

"Doesn't help us right now," he said.

"I have enough food to make us a meal," I said.

Shepherd's body tensed, and he kept his gaze on the ceiling as he said, "I know at work you want to keep this between you and me, which I understand, but I don't want to feel like I'm sneaking around in my personal life too. I don't want to stay inside and not go out to places or do things with you, Tristan. If that's how you're picturing our relationship, then maybe -"

"That's not it," I said.

"Then what is it?" Shepherd sat up when I did, resting one hand on my thigh. "Tell me."

"I'm broke, all right?" I said as shame made my cheeks burn. "I don't have the money to eat out."

"I'll pay for it," Shepherd said.

I raked my hand through my hair with frustration. "I'm already a charity case to Will. I don't want to be that to you too."

"How is me paying for a few meals make you a charity case?"

"It just does," I said.

"You need a better explanation than that," Shepherd said.

I scowled at him, and he leaned over and pressed a kiss against my forehead. "I don't mind, Tristan."

"I know you don't, but…"

"But what?"

"I'm not bad with money," I said. "I don't want you thinking I suck at managing my money. There were circumstances that…"

I didn't know how to finish the sentence. Getting into the business of my complicated relationship with my father wasn't something I wanted to share with Shepherd. Not this early in our relationship. Hell, I'd probably never share it.

Shepherd squeezed my leg. "Look, it's none of my business, Tristan. Don't worry about it, okay? But I do need you to accept that if I want to buy you food, I'm going to do it without any expectations or judgement."

I studied his face before rubbing my hand over the dark stubble on his jaw. He turned his head and kissed the palm of my hand. "I've been where you've been, all right? Like Nora said at the wedding, when Dad died, we weren't exactly swimming in money."

"What you did for your mom and your siblings was incredibly selfless."

He shrugged, his cheeks reddening a little. "They're my

family, and I love them. Any one of them would have done the same for me."

"When did you stop boxing?" I said.

"Just before I opened up the shop so about ten years ago," he said. "Ma took an evening payroll administrator course through a local college a few years before that, and she'd been working in payroll at her company for the last year and a half. She was making more money and she said she didn't need me taking a beating anymore just to pay for Davey's soccer trips."

"I thought you won most of your fights," I said.

"I did," Shepherd said. "But that doesn't mean I wasn't taking a beating in some of those fights. Anyway, Ma begged me to quit, said she was worried I'd be killed or suffer a brain injury. I was just about to open my own shop, and she and Nan said my business would suffer if clients walked in and saw my face messed up like I'd been in a bar fight."

"They weren't wrong," I said.

"They rarely are," Shepherd said. "Besides, I had to stop boxing once Ma played dirty and brought Nan into the conversation. She knows I do whatever Nan tells me to do."

"Well, I, for one, am very glad that your Nan has you wrapped around her baby finger. I like your face just like it is, and if you'd kept boxing, you wouldn't be nearly as pretty as you are." I gave him a lecherous grin and pinched his flat nipple.

He leaned in and kissed me, stealing my breath with the heat and the need that was in it. When we broke apart, he said, "You're going to pay for that pretty comment later tonight."

"Oh good, something to look forward to," I said.

He laughed and gave me a rough kiss on the side of the head. "C'mon, let's get in the shower."

CHAPTER 13

Shepherd

"For not being a vegan restaurant, this place has really good vegan food." Tristan set his fork down on the plate and took a drink of water.

"Yeah. Austin and I go here about twice a month," I said.

"That's your boxing trainer, right?" Tristan said.

"Yes. I don't box anymore, but we're still friends, and we hang out a lot. You'll like him. He's a good guy." Maybe the expectation that Tristan would meet Austin was too soon, considering we'd literally just decided to date two hours ago, but I didn't care. I hadn't dated anyone in a while, but when I decided to go in, I went all in.

"I'm looking forward to meeting him." Tristan gave me that grin, the one that made me believe he was the missing piece of puzzle I'd been searching for my entire life.

Warmth settled in my chest as I stared at Tristan's face. I'd only had a few serious relationships in my life and only been truly in love once. But I still recognized the emotion stirring inside of me. I was falling in love with Tristan. Hell, I *was* in love with him. Loving someone this quickly wasn't my usual MO, but how the fuck couldn't I love him? He was perfect.

"You okay?" Tristan said.

"Yeah, why?"

"You have a," he paused, "goofy look on your face."

I grinned at him. "I've never once been described as goofy looking before. I'm not sure if -"

"Tristan?"

Tristan's face lost all its colour, and the panicky look he gave me made every protective vibe in my body roar to life. I stared at the couple who had stopped at our table. The woman practically dripped in diamonds, and the guy had diamond cufflinks in his suit jacket and wore a Rolex on his wrist.

Tristan stood, one hand gripping the table for support. "Mom, Dad... what are you doing here?"

"The same as you, I would imagine," his father said. "Eating."

Tristan flushed with embarrassment before smiling at his mother. "You look nice today, Mom."

"Thank you." She smoothed her dress. "Your father just returned from Italy and brought this back for me."

"How was the trip?" Tristan said.

"Difficult and tiring," his father said. "I have way too much on my plate to be doing these kinds of trips, but since I'm the only one who cares about the family business, it all falls on me. But you're aware of that, aren't you, Tristan? You just don't care what it does to me. Because you're selfish and always have been."

The red faded from Tristan's face, leaving it the colour of dirty linen. My temper flared. I didn't know what the fuck his father's problem was, but I wasn't about to let him berate Tristan like a little kid in a restaurant full of people.

Before I could say anything, his mother turned to me and held out her hand. "I'm Cynthia Mills. You are?"

I stood and gave her hand a brief shake as Tristan said, "Sorry. Mom, Dad, this is Shepherd Hayes. He's a... friend. Shepherd, this is my mother Cynthia, and my father Peter."

"Nice to meet you." I had no desire to shake Tristan's father's hand, but I gritted my teeth and gave his hand a quick and perfunctory shake.

"Are you friends or," Cynthia's mouth made the slightest moue of disgust, "something more?"

"Something more," I said and took Tristan's hand.

I had no idea if he'd be pissed or happy that I was announcing our relationship to his parents, but I didn't give a fuck. I was riled up and ready to go to battle for him, and I wanted his parents to know that he had an ally.

"Isn't that nice," Cynthia said with a smile so fake it looked physically painful for her.

Tristan's hand clutched mine in a sweaty grip as an awkward silence fell over the four of us.

"Are you still coming for dinner next Sunday?" Cynthia said. She glanced at me but didn't extend the dinner invitation my way.

"Yes," Tristan said. "I'll be there."

His father's phone chimed, and Peter pulled it out from the inner pocket of his suit jacket. He studied the screen, his face darkening. "Oh, for the love of God."

"What's wrong?" Cynthia said.

"An issue at work. We can't stay to eat. I have to go into the office." He glanced at Tristan, the look on his face one of accusation and betrayal. "Some of us have the responsibility of an entire company on our shoulders and don't have the luxury of spending our Sunday relaxing with our loved ones."

If guilt had a picture in the dictionary, it would be Tristan's pale face. I squeezed his hand as he said, "Dad, I'm sorry. I know -"

"I don't have time for your apologies," Peter said. "It is what it is, and I've learned to live with your selfish behaviour. Cynthia, let's go."

He took his wife's hand, and she gave Tristan a brittle smile. "Enjoy your day off, Tristan."

Tristan swallowed hard. "Bye, Mom."

They walked away without saying anything else. Tristan watched them leave, the guilt etched into his face in heavy lines aged him about ten years. I squeezed his hand. "Tristan, you okay?"

"Fine," he said in a toneless voice that freaked me the fuck out.

He dropped my hand and sat down, staring blankly at his empty plate. I sat down and took his hand again. "Do you want to talk -"

"We should go," he said abruptly. "I have a headache and wouldn't mind lying down for a while."

"Sure," I said. My stomach tense and my worry for Tristan growing by the second, I caught the waiter's attention.

I FOLLOWED TRISTAN INTO HIS BEDROOM. HE HADN'T ASKED me to stay, but he hadn't demanded I leave either, even though he'd barely said a word to me on the way home. I had no idea if he was pissed at me or upset about his parents, but I was about to find out. I didn't play games in a relationship and I never would.

Tristan sat on the side of the bed, avoiding my gaze. I sat beside him and said, "Are you pissed at me?"

"No," he stared at the floor, "why would I be?"

"Because I told your parents we were dating, and it's obvious your mother doesn't approve of me."

"It's me and my choices she doesn't approve of," Tristan said. "You were just caught in the crossfire."

I took his hand. "So, your father is angry because you won't work at the family business?"

He nodded. "There's a little more to it, but yeah, that's basically it."

"Tell me the other parts of it," I said.

"It's a long story and boring and pointless." He reached over and placed his hand on my dick, rubbing lightly. "I can think of much more pleasant ways to spend the afternoon."

I took his hand and kissed the palm of it. "You know I want you, but using sex as a way to avoid talking about your feelings isn't a good idea."

He glanced at me and I was relieved to see the ghost of a smile on his face. "So, now you're my shrink, huh?"

"No, but I care about you, and it's obvious that your relationship with your parents is difficult. Talking helps. Trust me on this. I didn't want to talk about my dad dying, but I did, and it made a difference."

"Who did you talk to about your father passing away?" Tristan said.

"Nan, Austin, Connor… there's a long list," I said.

"My problem with my parents isn't as devastating as what you went through," Tristan said. "It's not -"

"It isn't a competition to see who has a more tragic back-story," I said. "Tell me why your father is such a dickhead."

Tristan's ghost of a smile grew. "Will's nickname for him is fuckwad."

"From our brief meeting today, I'd say his nickname for your father is fitting," I said.

Tristan took a deep breath before scooting back on the

bed and leaning against the wall. He patted the spot next to him. "Sit beside me and I'll tell you my pathetic life story."

I sat on the bed next to him, stretching my long legs out as Kevin jumped onto the bed. He was a brown tabby, and I studied the markings on his fur as he braced his front paws on Tristan's chest before purring and butting his face against Tristan's chin.

Tristan petted him absentmindedly with one hand and reached for mine with the other. I linked our fingers together and gave him an encouraging look as he stared at Kevin's face.

"My dad always struggled with being proud of me. He's a hard guy to impress, and nothing I did was ever good enough for him. I'm not the only one he treats that way, he's like that with all his employees, and his younger brother, and even my mom to a degree. I grew up used to being a disappointment to him."

He stroked along Kevin's back, smiling a little when the cat purred loudly. "My mom was never what you'd call affectionate, it's not in her nature, but she was proud of me. Until I came out as a teenager. She struggles with it a lot, even now."

"Your father was okay with it?"

He shrugged. "As far as he's concerned, it's just another way I've failed him and Mom. He didn't expect me to do anything right, so my attraction to guys was seen as simply another failure."

"You're not a failure," I said.

"You haven't heard the rest of the story yet," Tristan said as Kevin made a soft meow before jumping off the bed and strolling out of the bedroom.

I squeezed his hand, and after a few seconds of silence, Tristan went on. "My father has an insurance company called Mills Insurance."

I jerked. "That's the company I use to insure the shop and my personal shit too, like life and car."

Tristan nodded. "I'm not surprised. Mills Insurance is the largest insurance company in the county. I'd say at least seventy-five percent of the town has corporate or personal insurance coverage with us. Dad has a lot of big-name and wealthy clients, and he worked hard to get those clients. He built the company from the ground up, and he's put an enormous amount of time and sweat and effort into it. The success of the company is solely because of him, and I'm proud of what he's accomplished. I really am."

He glanced at me as if needing me to see that he was being truthful. I squeezed his hand again. "I know you are, Tristan."

"It was expected that I would join the business. I'm their only child and my father planned to pass the business onto me once he retired. He wants it to stay in the family. It being a family-owned business is a huge part of his marketing strategy."

"But you didn't want to go into insurance," I said.

"Not really. I loved cars. My grandpa on my mom's side was a mechanic. When I was little, he used to take me to classic car shows every summer. I loved it. I loved being in his shop, I loved the smells and the sounds and the grease on my grandpa's hands that never completely washed off."

He studied our hands clasped together. "My grandpa died when I was twelve. He was the only one in my family who understood me, and when he died…"

He swallowed hard and I moved a little closer, kissing the side of his head. "I'm sorry."

He cleared his throat. "Anyway, I didn't even consider becoming a mechanic. I went into the family business because I wanted Dad to be proud of me just one damn time. You know?"

I nodded, and Tristan stared at our clasped hands again. "I got my bachelor's degree in business, got my insurance license, and joined the company. Dad started me at the bottom as a junior agent, he said I didn't get a free ride just because I was his kid."

"Dickhead," I said.

Tristan shrugged. "I was fine with it. I wanted to prove to him that I could do it."

He lapsed into silence, and after a minute or so, I said, "You hated being an insurance agent."

"I did. But I also did well in the corporate world. I worked my way up to a senior agent in the firm pretty quickly. I've always been good with people, so clients loved me, and I brought in two really big clients. The combined yearly profit from them was close to a hundred grand. I worked a lot of hours and put in a massive amount of effort to bring those clients in. Do you know what my father said when I finally landed them, and they switched to our company?"

"What?" I said.

"He told me that I should have focused my attention on a different potential client because they would have ultimately landed a bigger profit for us."

"Fuck that guy," I said. "I know he's your dad, but he's an asshole."

Tristan stared across the room, his gaze hazy and his voice low. "It was then that I knew I'd never be able to please him. I had this vision of me in my fucking fifties, still trying everything I could to please my dad, and I… well, I kind of snapped. Will called it my mid-twenties life crisis."

"What did you do?" I said.

"I went in the next morning and quit. Told Dad that I was tired of living his dream and needed to start living mine. I told him I was taking the auto tech course and that I wanted his support."

"I bet he didn't take the news well," I said.

Tristan's laugh was bitter. "That's the understatement of the year. It was... bad. We both said a lot of hurtful things, and we didn't speak for about three months. He believes I've destroyed the company with my selfishness. That when he dies, the company will die with him."

"He can sell it to someone else," I said.

"He'd rather let it die," Tristan said.

"That's on him, not you."

"I know that in my head, but despite everything, there's still this stupid part of me that wants his respect. That wants him to acknowledge that I'm worthy of his love. But I'll never get it. I could work my fingers to the bone at Mills Insurance, and it wouldn't matter. He'll always find something to nitpick, something to be disappointed in me over. It's just his nature. And I know that, but it doesn't seem to make it any easier to stop," he made a frustrated sound in the back of his throat, "begging for his approval like a little kid."

He punched his own thigh. I took his hand, massaging and pulling on his fingers until he relaxed his hand. "It's normal for a kid to want his dad's approval, Tristan. What isn't normal is the way your dick of a father makes you jump through hoops to get it."

Tristan didn't reply, but his tense body relaxed a fraction, and he returned my kiss when I brushed my mouth against his.

"What happened then?" I asked.

"My dad thought if he shut me out that it would change

my mind. He wouldn't let my mom speak to me for the three months either."

"Fuck," I said under my breath.

"I applied for the auto tech program anyway. I made a good wage at my dad's company and I'd set aside some money. I used it to pay for the program and to cover my living expenses while I did it. Only…"

"Only what?" I said.

"When Dad realized that the silent treatment wasn't going to make me beg for my old job back, we started communicating again. I'd spent the last few years dreading every single morning because I had to go in to work. The relief I felt, the weight lifted off me was so…" he smiled a little, "I can't even explain how free I felt. It made me giddy, reckless… stupid."

"What do you mean?"

"I thought that because Dad could see how much happier I was in the auto tech program, that maybe he'd finally realized how much it meant to me. He hadn't brought up the family business since we started talking again, and he even asked me once how I liked the program."

Tristan's body was tensing again. "He didn't actually care. A few weeks after we started talking, he told me I needed to pay him back for the education he gave me since I was no longer using it."

"Pay him back?" I echoed.

"Mom and Dad paid my tuition and other school expenses when I got my bachelor's degree. It was a drop in the bucket for them. Financially they're set for life, and growing up, I never wanted for anything. My mom loves to travel, and I spent a good chunk of my childhood in Europe and Thailand and Australia."

"Seriously?" I said.

He nodded. "Yeah. I went to private schools and grew up in Abbotsdale."

"Holy shit," I said. Abbotsdale was the swankiest neighbourhood in our town. "Jack Walker lives in Abbotsdale."

"Yeah, I know. His house isn't that far from my parents' place," Tristan said.

"Are you telling me your parents are millionaires?" I said.

"Multi-millionaires," Tristan said.

"But they let you live in a crappy fucking apartment with barely any food," I said.

"My apartment isn't that crappy," Tristan protested.

"Bullshit," I said. "If Nan knew you were living here, she'd have my hide."

That made Tristan smile, and I'd be lying if his smile didn't calm some of my worry for him.

"Anyway, Dad wanted the money back that he and Mom invested in my education because I was no longer using it. A mechanic didn't need a bachelor's degree."

"Are you fucking kidding me?" I said in disgust.

"I wish I was. I didn't have the money, obviously, but Dad said that was fine, I could pay him in monthly instalments with interest. He knew it would fuck me over financially if I had this loan to pay him. He thought it would send me back to the family business."

Tristan shrugged. "It didn't. I don't love being broke all the fucking time, and I miss the apartment I had before this one, but... in the end, it's only stuff, right? After I finished the program, it took me a few months to get the job at your shop, and things got pretty bad financially. I was working in the car department at Walmart, but they paid fucking peanuts. With the loan payment to my dad, plus my rent, and just day-to-day expenses, I didn't have enough to cover. I sold my car and bought that embarrassing beater I drive around so I could pay my rent and cover the loan to Dad. The money from my car and my job at Walmart kept me from starving until Richie recommended me to you. He used to come into Walmart for car parts all the time. We sort of became friends, and when he asked if I wanted to make a bit of cash on the side by fixing his car, I said yes."

"My dad and Richie used to play pool together back in the day, and he kept in touch with Ma and the rest of us when Dad died. He knew I was looking for someone and recommended you. He said you were a genius with his car," I said.

Tristan smiled. "It was really great of him to do that. I thought I'd have to move to Riverton to find a job and I hated the idea. I'm not really a big city kind of guy."

He glanced at me. "It's why I was panicking when I fucked up at work. I really need this job to finish paying back my parents."

"Why do you give them the money?" I said. "You don't have to pay them back. Did they tell you at the time that if you didn't work for your father, you'd have to repay the tuition to them? Make you sign a contract or something?"

"No," Tristan admitted.

"Then fuck paying him back," I said. "What's he gonna do, sue you?"

Tristan laughed. "He might. Look, it's just easier to pay him what he thinks he's owed, all right? If I didn't pay him…"

"If you didn't pay him, what?" I said.

Tristan hesitated, and I squeezed his hand. "Tell me, baby."

"They're the only family I have. If I don't pay him, they'll cut off contact with me, and I'll be alone," Tristan said. "I don't have anyone else but Will and with him in a new relationship…" He shrugged. "I know my parents aren't great, but it's better than being completely alone."

I cupped his face and made him look at me. "You're not alone, Tristan. You have me and my awesome and completely insane family."

He smiled at me, but there was a sadness in it that made my chest ache. "Your family really is fantastic, Shepherd. I hope you know how lucky you are."

"I do," I said. "But I'm serious when I say they're your family now too. Okay?"

"We've only just started dating," he said. "Hell, they don't even know we're dating yet."

"True, but you've been to my sister's wedding. Mom has texted me three times to make sure I tell you that you're invited to all the Sunday family dinners from now on, and I know for a fact that Nora has been itching to ask you to go to some art show with her. You saw the way she almost had a heart attack at dinner when she realized you knew who that Italian artist she's obsessed with is… George Bellini or something."

Tristan smiled. "Giovanni Bellini."

"See," I said. "You fit right in with the Hayes family."

His smile widened and I leaned in and kissed him. "You have me now, Tristan. You'll never be alone again."

CHAPTER 14

Tristan

"Thank you for meeting me for lunch," Mom said. Her body tensed when I kissed her cheek before sitting across from her. I tried not to take it personally, she'd been like that my entire life. Showing her love for me in the form of touching wasn't her thing. I wondered if Shepherd knew how lucky he was to have a mom who was so free with her affection.

"What time do you have to be back to your little car fixing job?"

My mother probably didn't even hear the contempt in her voice.

"I don't work Mondays," I said. I studied the menu as my mother texted on her phone. She'd picked a barbeque joint. Even though she knew I was a vegan, I had no sense that she'd done it as punishment. She just rarely thought past her own wants and needs. If it wasn't for Clara, their personal chef, knowing I was vegan, I wouldn't have anything to eat at our sporadic family dinners.

"Have we decided what we're having?" The server stopped by our table with a bright smile and a shirt that said, *I like pork butts and I cannot lie.*

"I'll have the lunch platter special but with the pasta salad, not fries," my mother said without looking up from her phone.

"I'll have an order of fries," I said.

"Anything else, hon? The beef brisket is to die for."

"No, thank you," I said.

My mother frowned at me as the server left. "You really need to eat healthier, Tristan. Fries are terrible for you."

"So, what's up?" I said and took a sip of my water.

"Can't a mother just have lunch with her son?"

"Yes," I said. "So, what's new with you? Did you see they're doing an art exhibit at Paulson Gallery? I'm thinking of going with a friend, you're welcome to join us if you'd like."

"Your friend from yesterday?" My mother's voice went from annoyance to discomfort just like that.

"No, another friend. Her name is Nora. She's Shepherd's sister."

"Is Shepherd a friend of Will's?" Mom said. "I swear, Tristan, Will's always been such a bad influence on you. Introducing you to all sorts of... ideas and people."

"I was gay long before I met Will, Mom. You know that," I said.

"How long have you been dating Shepherd?"

"Not long, why?"

"He looks dangerous. I don't want you involved with someone who probably deals drugs."

I set my water down with a hard thump. "He doesn't deal drugs, Mom. Stop making assumptions about someone you don't even know."

"I'm looking out for your best interests," Mom said. "You're sweet and naïve, and you don't understand what kind of men are out there. If you would just consider dating a girl, maybe -"

I stood up. "I have to go. We've been over this a million times. I'm gay and that is never going to change."

"Tristan, wait!" My mother grabbed my wrist, smiling uncomfortably at the people seated at the table next to ours. "Sit down, please."

I sighed but sat down. "Look, I want to have lunch with you but not if you're going to bring up the subject of my sexuality."

"That isn't what I wanted to talk about," Mom said.

The server brought our food, and my mother waited until she left before unfolding her napkin and placing it on her lap. I ate a fry while Mom fiddled with her utensils.

I reached for another fry as Mom poked at her food.

"Your father has cancer."

I paused with the fry held in front of my mouth. "What?"

"Your father has been diagnosed with cancer."

"When? Where?" I said.

"A couple weeks ago. It's his back."

I dropped the fry and stared wide-eyed at my mother. "You found out Dad has spinal cancer a few weeks ago, and you're just telling me now?"

"This isn't about you,' she snapped before taking a deep breath and pressing on the bridge of her nose. "Your father didn't want anyone to know until we knew for sure that it was cancer."

"Okay, but I'm your kid," I said. "He's my father."

"I'm aware." She ate a few bites of food, but my throat had closed to a pinhole. I pushed the plate of fries away as my mother wiped her mouth.

"He's doing well, all things considered, but he'll be going in for surgery next month."

"Will he need to do chemo or radiation?" I said.

"It'll depend on the surgery," Mom said. She set her fork down and stared solemnly at me. "You know how proud your father is, and he would never say anything, but he's scared, and he needs your help."

"That's understandable," I said. "What can I do?"

"Come back to the company," she said.

My stomach churned and the single fry I ate threatened to come back up. "What?"

"The company needs you right now. Your father needs you. With this cancer diagnosis, he's not certain what will happen to the business. The stress he is under right now is unbelievable, Tristan." She reached across the table and took my hand, tears glinting in her eyes. "We need you, Tristan. *He* needs you. The thought of losing the business on top of the cancer… it's too much for him. You have to come back."

"Mom, I can't… I mean, I have a job, and I'm working toward finishing my apprenticeship. If I leave even for a few months to help Dad, it'll be impossible to find another job."

"Monkey." Mom's grip tightened on my hand. I couldn't remember the last time she'd called me the childhood nickname she'd given me. My throat burned, and I blinked rapidly as tears streaked down her face, ruining her perfect makeup job. "Your family needs you. I know things haven't always been easy between the three of us, but we're your parents and we love you. Your father pushed you so hard because he wants only the best for you, that's all. You walking away from the business broke his heart, Monkey. Please, do the right thing and come back to us. We need you. Will you help us, Tristan? Will you help your father?"

My voice hoarse, I said, "I will."

"You're quitting?" Shepherd sat down at the kitchen table with a heavy thump. "What the fuck do you mean you're quitting?"

I paced his small kitchen, my stomach in knots as I avoided Shepherd's gaze. "I'm putting in my notice. Friday is my last day."

"Friday is your… this Friday? This Friday is your last day?" Shepherd said.

I nodded, and he said, "What the fuck, Tristan? Is it because we're dating? Because I already told you that -"

"It's not because we're dating," I said.

"Then why?" Shepherd said. I could hear the frustration in his voice, but he gave me a calm enough look.

"I had lunch with my mother today. My father has cancer."

"Shit." Shepherd stood up and reached for me, and I allowed him to fold me into his embrace. "I'm sorry."

"Thanks. He's having surgery next month. Depending on how surgery goes will determine whether he needs chemo or radiation."

"Okay," Shepherd said cautiously, "but what does that have to do with you quitting?"

I took a deep breath. "I'm going back to work at the insurance company."

Shepherd stiffened against my body. "Are you fucking kidding me?"

"My father needs me," I said. "He's worried about what will happen to the company. My mother asked me to come back, to help Dad with the business while he has the surgery and recovers, and I said I would."

"What happens to the company isn't your problem,"

Shepherd said. "I'm sure there's someone else at the company who can look after things while your dad undergoes treatment."

I frowned at him and stepped back. "It's the family business, Shepherd. And after my dad, I know it better than anyone. I'm the right person for the job."

"But you hate working there," Shepherd said.

"It's not ideal, but he needs my help."

I could practically see the dark thunderclouds over Shepherd's head. Before he could say anything, I said, "He's my dad, Shepherd."

"He's treated you like shit your entire life."

"What does that have to do with anything?"

His look of exasperation got my back up. "Don't be deliberately obtuse, Tristan."

"I'm not," I snapped. "Look, I get that you don't approve of my decision, but this is happening. If it was your mother or your nan asking you for help, you'd upend your life to help them."

"Because they love me!" Shepherd shouted.

I winced. "But my father doesn't love me, is that what you're saying? I'm just such a fuck up that he couldn't possibly love me?"

"Stop it," Shepherd said. "Don't put fucking words in my mouth, Tristan. You know that isn't what I meant. You don't owe your father anything, not after what he's put you through. You think destroying your life, giving up everything you want because your old man has cancer, is the noble thing to do, but it isn't."

"It's not about being noble," I said. "It's about doing the right thing."

"This isn't the right thing," he said.

"I disagree."

He sighed and raked his hand through his hair. "So, what? You help your father until he recovers and then leave again. Is that it?"

"That's the plan. I talked to Dad on the phone after I had lunch with Mom, and he knows this is a temporary thing."

"I can't keep your job available for you," Shepherd said. "The shop is too busy, and I'll have to hire someone else to fill your position. The odds of me being able to hire you again later is slim to none."

"I know," I said. "I wasn't expecting you to keep my job waiting for me."

"You'll have to move to the city to finish your apprenticeship," Shepherd said.

"I know."

"What about us?"

I smiled tentatively at him. "I'm willing to do long distance, if you are?"

Shepherd paced the kitchen. "This is such fucking bullshit, Tristan. You're giving up your life again for a man who doesn't give a shit about you. He doesn't deserve the sacrifice you're making for him. You can't do this."

"I am," I said.

"What kind of cancer does he have?"

"Spinal," I said. "He says it hasn't spread from his back yet, and hopefully the surgery he has next month will keep it from spreading."

"So, he's having a tumour removed?" Shepherd said.

"I think so."

"What do you mean, you think so?" Shepherd said.

"We didn't get into specifics. Dad doesn't like to talk about personal shit all that much."

Shepherd studied me. "Tristan, are you sure your dad

even has cancer? Maybe this is just another fucked up way of trying to control you?"

I stared at Shepherd, my shock so great, I was completely speechless.

"It's not out of the realm of possibility, right?" Shepherd continued to pace, his voice picking up steam as he warmed to his idea. "I mean, he's desperate to keep the family business going, and he's not getting any younger. You've told him before that you're never coming back, but he knows you. He knows your weakness. He's using that weakness to get what he wants."

He glanced up at me, his frantic pace slowing to a stop, his hands reaching for me. "Tristan? What is it? What's wrong?"

I stepped away from him, backing up until I was in the kitchen doorway. "Weakness? Since when did compassion and love for family become a weakness?"

"I didn't mean it like that. I just meant -"

"I know exactly what you meant," I said. "You think my father is a monster, and I'm spineless and weak and will do whatever he tells me to do."

"No, that isn't it."

"That's what you just said," I replied. I held up my hand when he tried to protest. "No, don't bother, Shepherd. You know, I've never told anyone other than Will about what a failure my father thinks I am. Never told anyone how... how broken I feel or how lonely I've been. But then you... I... I thought I could trust you with my heart. I was wrong."

"Baby, you can trust me," Shepherd said. "I only want what's best for you."

"Do you? Or do you want what's best for you? Because the way I see it, me working at the shop and sleeping in your bed benefits you more than it does me."

Shepherd's face paled and I immediately regretted my words. "Shepherd, I didn't mean that. I'm just... I'm fucked up right now, okay? My dad is sick, and I could really use your support."

I swallowed down the hellish lump in my throat when Shepherd said, "It was a mistake for us to date. You should go, Tristan."

"Fine," I said. "You want to bail on our relationship at the first road bump, go right ahead."

"This is more than a fucking road bump, and you know it!" Shepherd shouted. "This is your father destroying your fucking life, and you sitting back and letting him do it!"

I grabbed my jacket from the back of the chair. "That's your opinion."

"That's the truth," Shepherd said. "Don't bother coming in the rest of the week."

"Are you firing me?" I said. "Because I've already quit, remember?"

"I remember. I'll pay you out to Friday and have Roger pack up your shit and drop it by your place. Don't show your face at my shop again, Tristan."

"I won't." Dangerously close to vomiting, I walked out of Shepherd's house and didn't look back.

CHAPTER 15

Shepherd

"Shepherd?" Both Marybeth's knock on the door and her voice were timid.

I couldn't blame her. I'd been a right bastard the last four weeks, and I was extremely lucky she, as well as Roger and Gurdeep, hadn't outright quit.

"Yeah?" I looked up from my laptop where I'd been pretending to order parts but was mostly just thinking about Tristan and how badly I'd fucked up.

"There's a Will Matthews here to see you."

The name sounded vaguely familiar. I glanced over today's work orders on my desk but didn't see his name. "Did he drop off a car this morning?"

"No." Marybeth cleared her throat. "He says he's a friend of Tristan's."

I froze, my hand clenching compulsively around a work order, the sound of the paper crinkling the only noise in the room.

After a moment, Marybeth said, "Should I tell him you're busy or…"

"No, I'll see him. Can you bring him back to my office?" My voice was hoarse, and my hand was shaking a little as I smoothed out the work order and placed it back on my desk.

"Sure," Marybeth said.

"Marybeth?" She paused in the doorway and I said, "I'm sorry for being such a fucking dick the last month."

She smiled a little. "That's all right. I know how much you miss Tristan." She left before she could see the way my mouth dropped open.

I heard footsteps in the hallway, and a tall dark-haired man wearing dress pants and a collared shirt stepped into my office. "Mr. Hayes? I'm Will Matthews."

I shook his hand and indicated toward the crappy folding chair in front of my desk. "Call me Shepherd."

He sat down and there were a few seconds of awkward silence before he said, "I'm Tristan's best friend."

"I know. He's mentioned you."

"He's mentioned you a lot," Will said.

His dark eyes revealed nothing of what I wanted to know. I cleared my throat. "How's he doing?"

"He's miserable. He misses you," Will said bluntly.

"He's the one who left," I said.

Will gave me a look that could have melted concrete. "You know he had no choice."

"He had a choice. He could have stayed here with me – I mean, the shop, where he was happy, but he didn't. He chose to help a man who will never have any fucking idea how amazing Tristan is."

"Look, Tristan's dad is a fucking piece of work, I'm not disagreeing with you, but the man is Tristan's father, and he has cancer. Did you really think Tristan wouldn't help him? Tristan is -"

"Kind," I said. "He's kind and... good and the best fucking man I know."

"He is," Will said. "And you went and broke his heart."

"He broke mine too," I said.

"It's not a fucking competition," Will said.

"Yeah, I know."

"Tristan needs you right now," Will said.

"Is that what he said?"

"Not in so many words, but," Will shook his head at the look on my face, "he does. Just because he refuses to admit it, doesn't mean it isn't true. Working at the insurance company, being under his father's thumb again, for even just the last month, it's done a real number on him. If you care about him, then you'll respect the choice he's made and still be a part of his life."

"I love him," I said. I hadn't meant to say it, it had just fallen out of my mouth, but I felt an immeasurable amount of relief at saying those three little words.

"Good. Because I've known Tristan for a really long time, and it's easy to see that he's in love with you," Will said.

"I'm not sure I can watch his father destroy his life without saying anything," I said.

Will leaned forward, resting his elbows on his knees and staring intently at me. "I get it. I hate it too, and there have been a few times this last month where I've been unsuccessful at biting my tongue around Tristan when it comes to his father. But you being supportive, even with the occasional slip-up, will mean the world to Tristan."

He glanced at his watch and stood. "I have to get back to the school before lunch ends. It was good to meet you, Shepherd."

"Good to meet you too." I stood and shook Will's hand, sinking back into my chair when he left my office.

I stared blankly at the work orders on my desk. I missed Tristan. I could barely sleep or eat the last few weeks, and I'd done nothing outside of work other than family dinners. I'd missed so many workouts at the gym that Austin had dropped by my place to see if I was still alive. I was so miserable at family dinners that Eva had started referring to me as "Sad Uncle Shepherd."

I leaned back in my chair, closing my eyes and rubbing at my forehead. Knowing Tristan was as miserable as I was didn't make me feel any better. In fact, it made me feel worse.

I didn't know what the fuck I was going to do, but I did know I couldn't keep denying how much I missed Tristan. Something had to change.

Tristan

I knocked on my father's office door before stepping inside. "Dad, do you have a minute to talk?"

"Not really," my father said irritably. "I'm meeting with Andrew to go over the Henderson account in five minutes."

"Oh, I've already met with Andrew and gave him the information he needed."

My father's face turned red. "What?"

I nodded. "I was meeting with him earlier about the Frost account, so went over the Henderson stuff as well."

"The Henderson is my account," my father said.

"Yes, but I know you have a lot on your plate, and with your surgery coming up, I thought it would be helpful if -"

My father stood. "I appreciate that you've come back to

the family business, Tristan, but don't forget that it's still *my* business. This cancer nonsense doesn't mean I'm just going to hand the company over to you and let you run it into the ground."

I frowned at him. "I know that. I'm just trying to help. That's what you asked me to do, so let me do it."

"There's a difference between helping and hindering," Dad said. "You fucked up on the Franklin account yesterday."

"How?" I said.

"The policy is wrong. They didn't want their workshop included in the coverage, and you put it on there."

"One, the Franklins made a last minute decision to include the workshop and asked me to modify the policy, so I did. And two, how do you know it was on the policy?" I said. "The Franklin account is mine. I brought it in last week."

My father sighed loudly. "Obviously, I'm going to be looking over your work, Tristan. I can't trust that you'll do everything correctly when you've been letting your brain sit idle while you tinker with broken cars. You made a ton of mistakes when you'd been working at the company for years. I expect it to be worse now that you've forgotten most of what you learned here."

I gritted my teeth and forced myself to stay calm. "I haven't forgotten what I've learned, and I haven't made any mistakes. You don't need to babysit me, all right? I'm here to help you while you recover."

My father made a disinterested grunt before sitting back down. Taking a deep breath, I sank into the chair across from his desk. "Do you have the date for your surgery yet? It should be happening soon, right?"

"I'm meeting with the doctor tomorrow." My father looked away, staring at his screen and tapping on the keyboard in front of him. "I'll have more information then."

"More information on when the surgery is?" I said.

My father made an annoyed sound in the back of his throat as he leaned in and studied the screen. "Oh, for God's sake, Jasmine screwed up the supply order again. She's incredibly incompetent, and if she fucks up again, I'm firing her."

"Dad," I said. "How big is the tumour they're removing? Do you have an idea of recovery time?"

He stared impatiently at me. "Tristan, I've already told you I'm busy. Can we please talk about personal things outside of work? Maybe at that garage you worked at, it was perfectly fine to charge customers money while you sat around and gossiped like women, but we have a better work ethic at Mills Insurance. I hope you remember that in twenty-five years when I've retired and you're in charge."

"This is a temporary thing," I said. "I'm not staying permanently, and you know that, Dad."

"Yes, yes," he waved his hand impatiently. He'd already returned to staring at his screen. "Is that all, Tristan? I have a lot of work to do."

I stood and left his office, pulling at my collar as I walked down the hall toward mine. My tie was too tight, and my suit felt too restrictive, and I would have done anything to be back in my oil-stained coveralls.

My stomach clenched, and I tried to ignore the nausea swirling in it. I'd been sick to my stomach since the night Shepherd and I broke up, and I didn't foresee that changing any time soon. It made eating nearly impossible, and the amount of coffee I'd been drinking would give me a damn ulcer if I wasn't careful.

Not in the mood to be chatty, I was grateful not to run into any coworkers before I made it to my office. I sank into the leather chair and loosened the tie around my neck before staring moodily at my computer screen. I was miserable, but I was trying to concentrate on helping my father and not obsessing over how much I hated my job and how much I missed Shepherd.

Even just thinking his name brought on a wave of loneliness. Fuck, I missed him so much. Any anger I'd felt over what he'd said had faded a long time ago. Now all I could think about was how much I wanted to hear his deep voice again, touch his warm skin, press my lips against his. The last four weeks had been the longest and most difficult of my life, and I spent every evening telling myself not to text him. I was showering poor Kevin with so much attention that he'd taken to hiding in the linen closet for a good portion of the evening, desperate for a little alone time.

My phone rang. The call was from reception, and I picked up the receiver. "Hey, Martha. What's up?"

"Hi, Tristan. I have a Judith and Nora Hayes here to see you. They don't have an appointment, but your calendar is empty so I thought I'd check to see if you –"

"Yes!" I blurted out. "Yes, I can see them."

Martha was momentarily silenced by the obvious eagerness in my voice. "All right. Jenny's right here, I'll ask her to bring them back to your office on the way to hers."

"Thanks." I hung up the phone and stupidly tightened my tie and smoothed my hair before grabbing a mint from my desk and crunching it down. I didn't know why I was nervous or what I was expecting, but just the thought of seeing someone who knew Shepherd filled me with a combination of anticipation and excitement.

There was a knock on my door before it opened and Shepherd's nan and Nora stepped inside. I hurried around my desk, nodding my thanks to Jenny as she closed the door behind them.

"Nan, Nora, it's... it's so good to see you." I hesitated before holding out my hand.

Nan made a face and opened her arms. "You know I'm a hugger, Tristan."

My eyes watering, I hugged Nan, blinking hard and trying not to crush her with my enthusiasm. When she released me, I turned toward Nora, who threw her arms around me and kissed my cheek.

"You look as terrible as Shepherd does," she said.

"Nora," Nan said. "Hush now, dearest."

"He does, Nan," Nora said. The pink streaks in her hair were now purple, and she had a new piercing in her eyebrow.

"Is he okay?" I said. "Is Shepherd..."

"He's physically fine, sweetheart, don't you worry now."

"How did you know I was working at my father's insurance company?" I said.

"Shepherd told us." Nan patted my hand before slipping it into the crook of my elbow. "Would you mind if I sat down? It was a bit of a walk from the parking lot to your building."

"Of course, I'm so sorry for my bad manners." I walked her over to the chairs in front of my desk and helped her ease into it as Nora sat down in the other.

"Thank you, dear Tristan," Nan said.

"Can I get you a glass of water?" I said.

"No, no, you sit down. You look as tired as I do," Nan said.

Knowing I looked a little ridiculous but not caring, I pushed my chair out from behind my desk and rolled it over to Nan's. I wanted to sit beside her without a desk between us. I wanted to be close to her not just because of how much I missed Shepherd, but because I'd missed her too. I missed all of Shepherd's family.

I sat down and took Nan's hand. "How's your arm?"

"Oh, good." Nan flexed her opposite arm. "Got the cast off just last week, and the doctor says my arm is as good as new."

"I'm glad to hear it," I said.

"This is a pretty fancy office," Nan said.

I just shrugged. "I'm really glad to see you two."

"We're happy to see you too," Nora said. "Davey and I actually fought over who would drive Nan to your office."

"You won, huh?" I said with a small smile.

"Yeah. I fight dirty, so Davey didn't have a chance." She grinned at me before sobering. "I'm sorry to hear about your dad. Shepherd told us about his diagnosis. How's he doing?"

"Okay," I said. "It hasn't slowed him down at all. But he hasn't had surgery yet."

"You're a good boy for helping him the way you are," Nan said. She studied my face. "I'll be honest, I don't know why Shepherd's so upset that you're helping him. He's always put his family first, so it's a bit hypocritical of him to be angry that you're doing the same."

"He didn't tell you," I said.

"He hasn't really told us anything beyond your father has cancer and you quit the garage to work in the family business again. Not even Connor knows more than that, and Shepherd usually tells him everything," Nora said.

"My dad and I have had our struggles in the past," I said. "He's, uh, very demanding and has high expectations."

"Fathers can sometimes be too hard on their boys," Nan said. "I'm sure it comes from a place of love, but it doesn't make it any easier to bear."

"I love him, I do, but our relationship is... difficult."

Nan squeezed my hand. "Did you and Shepherd break up because your father doesn't approve of you being gay?"

"No, that wasn't it. We broke up because..."

My throat burned and I could feel the sting of tears at the back of my eyes. "Because I'm an idiot."

"Oh, I know that's not true," Nan said. "My grandson has never been one to suffer fools, and if you were an idiot, he would never have hired you to work at the garage."

"We got into a fight when I said I had to quit and we… he…"

"Did he shout at you?" Nan said. "Sometimes he shouts."

I couldn't help but smile. "A little, but I think I was shouting too."

"Well, sometimes even two people who love each other as much as the two of you do will shout. It can't be helped. No relationship is perfect," Nan said.

"Shepherd doesn't love me," I said.

"Oh, please." Nora rolled her eyes. "Shepherd is ridiculously in love with you. It's kind of gross how much he loves you. Like, I half expect to see little hearts come busting out of his eyeballs whenever we even mention your name. Which we do a lot because we miss you and we hate seeing Shepherd so sad. We had a family meeting the other night without Shepherd where the consensus was that Shepherd's being ridiculous and so are you, and we needed to do something about it."

She glanced at Nan. "So, here we are. Doing something about it."

"Here you are," I repeated softly.

"We voted for Nan to be the one to talk to you because no one can resist doing what she tells them to do," Nora said with a cheeky grin. "It's, like, a sin to disobey Nan."

"Hush now, Nora," Nan said, but there was a smile on her wrinkled face. "I'm not going to tell Tristan what to do. He's a grown man who can make his own choices in life. But I am going to say that my grandson loves you and misses you, and

I think if the two of you talk, you'll realize that while family is important, being with the one you love is what matters. You love Shepherd and he loves you, and it breaks my heart to see the two of you apart."

"You're breaking an old woman's heart," Nora said solemnly, but her eyes were sparkling with mischief. "Can you live with that, Tristan?"

"Who are you calling an old woman?" Nan said. "I'm still young and hip. Why, just the other night Widow Gallagher texted me a picture of his penis."

Nora's mouth dropped open. "Eighty-seven-year-old Mr. Gallagher from down the street? He did not send you an unsolicited dick pic, Nan."

"It wasn't unsolicited, dear," Nan said with a serene smile.

I burst into laughter as Nora made a face. "Oh my God, my grandma's getting dick pics from men. I don't know if I should be impressed or jealous."

"Oh, trust me, Widow Gallagher is a sweet man, but his penis is nothing to be jealous about. Mr. Trustman's though..." Nan fanned her face, "that man is blessed in the penis department."

"Mr. Trustman?" Nora's eyes widened. "Horace Trustman... the guy who runs Bingo night at the community center?"

"That's the one," Nan said.

"Nan," Nora said, "how many men are sending you dick pics?"

Nan smiled. "A lady never kisses and tells, dearest. But this isn't about me. This is about Tristan and Shepherd, and how much they miss each other. Will you call Shepherd, dear Tristan?" Nan squeezed my hand again. "Just to talk to him?

He's been so upset, and I know it would do him a world of good to hear your voice again."

I swallowed hard before nodding. "If you think that's what he really wants, yes, I'll call him."

"He'll be so happy." Nan smiled at him. "Thank you, Tristan."

"Thank you." My voice was hoarse again, and Nan must have seen the emotion on my face because she leaned forward and cupped my face.

"It will all work out, sweetheart. I know it will."

I nodded, my ability to talk had flown out the window, and Nan smiled again. "Now, we've taken up enough of your time, so we'll go, but I appreciate you seeing us in the middle of your work day."

I cleared my throat. "It was my pleasure, Nan. I'm really glad to see you."

Nan stood and took Nora's hand. "You're part of our family now, Tristan. Don't ever forget that."

CHAPTER 16

Tristan

I studied my cell phone. In the last half hour since Nan and Nora had left, I'd wavered between calling Shepherd immediately or waiting until the end of the day. I wanted to call him now, wanted to hear his voice and hope like hell that Nan was right about him being happy to hear mine. But I also knew that Thursdays were one of the busier days in the shop.

Before I could make up my mind, there was a knock on my door, and a small and trim gray-haired woman stepped into my office.

"Aunt Linda?" I stood up and hurried across the room, sweeping the older woman into a tight hug. "Hi! I didn't know you were here."

"I just flew in this morning." My aunt took a step back, holding my arms and looking me up and down. "You look sad, Tristan. What's wrong?"

"I'm fine," I said. "Don't worry about me. It's so good to see you. It's been almost two years."

"I know, but I've been so busy with the farm, and most

of the time your mother travels to see me. Your mom picked me up at the airport this morning. We just finished lunch over at Mercutio's and decided to pop in since the office is so close. She's chatting to your father and I thought I'd stop in and see my favourite nephew now that you're working here again."

I laughed. "I'm your only nephew."

"Doesn't make you any less my favourite." She pinched my cheek, making me laugh again.

My mother's sister was as different from my mother as night was from day. Growing up, my favourite memories were the ones spent with my grandfather at his garage and the occasional vacations I'd spent at my aunt and uncle's farm when my parents went on a trip without me.

"Is Uncle Dave here too?"

"Oh, God no. You know it's like pulling teeth to get him to leave the farm."

"Is he still saving animals at the auction and finding them good homes?"

Aunt Linda laughed. "Of course he is. He brought home a llama the other day. A llama! He said he's going to find him a new home, but between you and me, I'm pretty sure the damn thing's already found its home right there on the farm."

"Well, I'm really glad to see you. Mom can use all the support she can get for Dad's upcoming surgery."

Aunt Linda blinked at me. "Upcoming surgery?"

I stared at her in confusion. "Didn't Mom tell you?"

"Tell me what?" she said.

"Dad has cancer," I said slowly. Bile was churning in my belly and in the back of my head. I could hear Shepherd's voice asking if I was sure Dad had cancer.

"Oh, that." Aunt Linda made a 'no big deal' motion with her hand. "No, I'm not here because of the cancer thing. I was just missing your mom, that's all. Besides, your mom said the surgery was last week and everything went fine."

"What? Dad hasn't had the surgery yet," I said.

"He has," Aunt Linda said. "I talked to your Mom the day of the surgery. It was," she thought for a minute, "Wednesday morning. She was at the hospital."

"That's not possible," I said. "Dad was out of the office Wednesday morning, but he was here that afternoon."

Aunt Linda shrugged. "Well, it wasn't exactly an invasive surgery, was it? Your mom said they didn't even put him under. Just some freezing to the area and a few sutures and he was good to go. Your mom said he gets the results from the biopsy tomorrow."

"There's no way he had a tumour removed from his spine with some freezing and a few sutures," I said.

"Tumour removal?" Aunt Linda gave me a startled look. "What tumour?"

"From Dad's spine," I said. "He has spinal cancer. It's a tumour. Isn't it?"

"Is that what he told you?" My aunt looked as confused as I felt.

"Well, no, not exactly. Mom said they'd found cancer in his back, and I just assumed it was a tumour. They haven't really given me much information. You know how Dad is when it comes to talking about personal stuff." My heart was thudding, and every nerve in my body was screaming at me that something was very wrong.

"Sweetie, your dad doesn't have spinal cancer. He has skin cancer."

"Skin cancer," I repeated. "Are you sure?"

"Yes," Aunt Linda said. "I'm positive. He had a strange mole on his back, and they did a biopsy and confirmed it was cancerous. The surgery he had last week was to remove the mole and some of the surrounding tissue. He finds out tomorrow if that's removed it all or if he'll need to do radiation, but the doctor said that he's, like, ninety-nine percent confident the surgery will be enough."

"So… it's not a tumour on his spine," I said.

"Definitely not," Aunt Linda said. She made a startled sound when I suddenly pushed past her. "Tristan? Where are you going?"

I didn't answer. I strode down the hallway toward my father's office, my quick pace turning into a run. By the time I reached his office and threw open the door, I was panting from a combination of cardio and the rage building slowly inside of me.

My mother made a startled scream when I slammed the door so hard behind me that a picture fell off the wall and the glass smashed when it hit the floor.

"What the hell, Tristan?" my father said.

"You lied to me." I stalked toward his desk. "You fucking lied to me."

"Watch your mouth," Dad said.

I slammed my hand down on his desk. "Skin cancer? You have fucking skin cancer, Dad?"

He glanced at my mother before standing and straightening his shoulders. "I never said it was spinal cancer. You made an assumption Tristan, and that's not on me."

I turned to my mother. "That day at the restaurant, you knew I was misunderstanding what you told me, and you didn't say anything. Why? I expect that kind of shit from Dad, but not from you."

My mother already had tears streaming down her face, but I ignored them. "Tell me, Mom."

"Because you were – were with that terrible man!" she said. "He's no good for you, Tristan. I knew he was your boss, you know. I looked up Hayes Garage when you first started working there, and I saw his picture on the website. I knew the only way to get you away from him was if you stopped working for him. I was only trying to do what was best for you."

"No!" I shouted. "You weren't! You were trying to turn me into the person you want me to be! Well, guess what? I'm not that person, and I never will be. I won't marry a woman and have a dozen grandkids for you, Mom. I like men and I always will. And all you've done with your lies is ensure that when I do have kids, they'll never know their grandmother."

"Stop it," she said. "I didn't lie to you. You misunderstanding what I said doesn't mean I lied to you."

"Don't," I said. "Don't try to fucking justify your shitty behaviour."

"Enough!" my father roared. "You will not speak to your mother that way, Tristan. Do you hear me? I won't stand for it! Apologize to her, right now."

Bitter laughter spilled out of me. "The days of me doing what you say are long over, Dad. You've used me and manipulated me into getting what you wanted for most of my life, and it's over. Do you hear *me*? I'm done."

"You're so selfish," my father spat. "This company means everything to me, and you've never cared about that or about -"

"Fuck this company!" I shouted. "The company means more to you than your own goddamn son, and you know what? For a long time, I thought it was because of me. That because I could never be the person you wanted to be, and I was never good enough or smart enough for you, that it was my fault you cared more about the fucking company than you did about me."

My father opened his mouth, and I slammed my hand on

the desk again. "No! I'm not interested in hearing what other lies will spew from your mouth. There is nothing wrong with me. There is nothing wrong with being a mechanic, and I won't let you convince me that there is. One of the smartest men I know is a mechanic, and I'm proud to know him and to work for him."

I glanced at my mother. "I'm proud to be his boyfriend."

"Tristan," she said. "You don't -"

"This conversation is done," I said and walked toward the door of my father's office. I paused in the doorway and stared at my parents. "I'm not paying you another cent for my tuition. You can sue me if you want the money. Oh, and I quit. Do me a favour and lose my number. I don't want to talk to either of you ever again."

"We're your family," my mother said. "We're the only ones you have, Tristan."

I shook my head. "You couldn't be more wrong."

Shepherd

"SHEPHERD, ARE YOU LISTENING TO ME?"

I stared blankly at Roger sitting across from me before shaking my head. "No, sorry."

He rolled his eyes. "Look, I get that you're going through a rough time right now, but if you'd just fucking talk to Tristan and tell him how you feel, you'd be a lot less miserable."

I stared at him. "Does everyone in this goddamn shop know about me and Tristan?"

"It's kind of impossible to ignore when you're making googly eyes at him all day."

"I was not making… googly eyes," I said. "I'm a grown fucking man, Roger."

"Whatever," he said. "Look, I don't know why Tristan quit, but I do know you've been a right fucking shithead since he left. You need to talk to him."

"I'm your boss, Roger. Maybe watch the tone."

He just shrugged. "You might be able to scare poor Marybeth and Gurdeep with that attitude, but I've known you a long fucking time. I'm more than just your damn employee, Shepherd. We're friends, aren't we?"

"Yeah," I said. "We're friends."

"And I'm telling you as your friend that Tristan is the best damn thing to ever happen to you. So, get off your ass and drive to that stupid insurance company he said he was going to be working for, and tell him how you feel."

"Right now," I said.

"Right fucking now."

"I've got shit to do here," I said.

"Shit that me or Gurdeep could do, and you know it," Roger said. "Get the hell out of here and go talk to Tristan."

I stared at him before standing abruptly and pushing my chair back. "Okay."

"Thank Christ," Roger said. "I thought we were going to have to do an intervention to get you to -"

The door to my office banged open, and I stared in surprise at Tristan as he marched into the room. He was wearing a dark suit that clung to his broad shoulders. The tie was pulled loose around his neck, and the top few buttons of his shirt were undone. He looked a little bit angry and a whole lot sexy as he stopped in front of me.

"Tristan, I -"

His hands cupped my face and his mouth landed on mine. He kissed me with an urgent, bruising pressure, his tongue pushing at my lips. At the first touch of his mouth after nearly a month, I suddenly didn't give one fuck that we were at work or that Roger was in the office with us.

I pulled him up tight against me, sliding my hand around the back of his neck and angling my mouth over his. I took the kiss deep, our tongues sliding together, our teeth clashing as Tristan dropped his hands to my waist and wrapped his arms around me. I pulled back, sucking in a breath of air as my lips tingled.

"I love you," Tristan said, his gaze never leaving mine. "I love you, Shepherd."

"I love you too," I said.

"I'm sorry. You were right, and I'm so fucking sorry."

I shook my head and pressed my forehead against his. "Stop. Don't apologize. I'm the one who's sorry."

He kissed me again before saying, "Fuck, I've missed you."

"I've missed you too." I smiled at him, my heart pounding when Tristan returned my smile.

"You two are fucking adorable," Roger said.

Tristan jerked before turning to stare at Roger. "Oh, uh, hey, Roger."

"Hey, Tristan." Roger grinned at him.

"Sorry," Tristan said to me as he started to step away. I tightened my grip on him, refusing to release him. "If you're not busy tonight, maybe I could stop by and we can talk?"

This time it was me who stepped away, but the look of disappointment on Tristan's face disappeared when I grabbed his hand and pulled him toward the door. "Roger, I'm taking the rest of the day off. Don't call me if there are any problems."

Roger laughed. "Wouldn't dream of it, boss."

"So, HE DOES HAVE CANCER, JUST NOT SPINAL CANCER." I stared at Tristan as I handed him the glass of water.

"Skin cancer. And, according to my Aunt Linda, it's not even that serious. He had surgery last week to remove the mole and finds out tomorrow if he needs radiation."

"Christ,' I said. "What an asshole."

"Right?" Tristan drank a few swallows of water.

"What happens if he does need radiation?" I said.

Tristan shrugged. "Not my problem."

"Tristan, I don't -"

He took my hand and squeezed it. "Hey, my relationship with my parents is finished. I don't know if it's finished permanently or if in a few years, I'll be in a better space to forgive them for what they've done, but for now... I'm done with them. They don't deserve to have me in their lives."

"No, they don't," I said. "I'm sorry that they lied to you."

"Me too, but I should have expected it. I should have listened to you, and I never should have left."

"Don't do that," I said. "Don't beat yourself up for the choice you made. Wanting to help your family was the right thing to do, and I'm sorry for the shit I said. Sorry that I made you feel awful for wanting to help them."

He smiled and leaned forward to press a kiss against my mouth. "Thanks, honey. I just wish I'd listened to you in the first place. I'm sorry for what I said about our relationship benefiting you more. I didn't mean it and I shouldn't have said it. You are the best thing that's ever happened to me, and I love you."

"I love you too," I said. "So, now what?"

"Well, now I start looking for a shop in Riverton willing to take on an apprentice," Tristan said. "I know long distance relationships are hard, but would you be open to giving it a try? I don't want to lose you, but I really want to finish my apprenticeship and -"

"Tristan," I said, "you can have your job back at the shop."

He stared at me in surprise. "It's been a month. You had to have hired someone to replace me."

"I haven't," I said. "I couldn't."

"Are you serious?"

"Yes," I said.

"But..." he studied me over the rim of his water glass, "Roger saw us kiss. He knows that -"

"They all know," I said. "Marybeth, Roger, Gurdeep... the whole fucking shop knows I'm head over heels for you."

A grin was turning up his lips. "Probably because you keep looking at me like you want to fuck me."

"I do want to fuck you," I said. "Also, Roger was a bit politer and called it me making googly eyes at you."

Tristan burst into laughter, and the pure joy in the sound made happiness flood my body for the first time in weeks. "Oh my God, that's hilarious."

"Anyway, they all know we're dating, and even if they didn't, you're still working at the shop. I can't go another fucking day without seeing you."

"Same here," Tristan said. "Thank you, Shepherd."

I studied him. "Will came to see me."

"Will... my best friend Will came to see you?" Tristan said.

"Yes. At lunch time today. He was worried about you. He asked me to talk to you, said you were unhappy and that you missed me."

"He was right," Tristan said.

"I was going to stop by your place after work," I said. "I

was going to tell you that I was on your side whether you worked for your father or not and that I was sorry, and that I missed you and loved you."

Tristan laughed so hard that he spilled some of his water.

"That's funny to you?" I arched an eyebrow at him in mock disapproval, but I was only teasing. I loved his laugh. Had missed his laugh.

"Nan and Nora came to see me today just after lunch," Tristan said.

"What?"

"I guess they had a family meeting and -"

"They had a family meeting without me?"

"Yes. Anyway, they had the meeting and decided that we were both being ridiculous, and someone needed to talk to me. They voted for Nan to be the one to tell me I needed to talk to you."

"Of course they did," I said. "No one can resist doing what Nan asks."

"It is a remarkable superpower she has," Tristan said. "Anyway, it was just… it was wonderful to see them again, and it made me realize how stupid I was being. It really didn't take much convincing from Nan for me to agree to talk to you. I was going to stop by your place after work."

Now it was my turn to laugh, and Tristan grinned at me. "How hilarious would it have been if you were at my crappy apartment and I was here at your place?"

He reached for my hand again. "Anyway, then I found out about my parents lying to me, and you know the rest… and now here we are."

"Here we are." I studied his gorgeous face, the one I had missed so fucking much the last four weeks. "Move in with me."

"What?"

"Move in with me," I repeated. "The last four weeks without you have been fucking hell. I don't want to spend another minute without you in my life."

"If we live together, that means we spend all day together and all evening," he said. "Is that what you really want?"

"Yes. You don't?"

"I'm good with it," he said. "More than good with it."

"Then it's not a problem. You can move in this weekend."

I leaned forward to kiss him, stopping when Tristan said, "Kevin."

"What about him?"

"He's moving in too."

"Obviously," I said. "It'll be kind of difficult for him to attack my ass if he's still living at your apartment."

Tristan laughed, and I pressed a kiss against his throat. "What do you say we head to my bedroom? I want to show you how much I've missed you."

"I like that idea," Tristan said. "Also, this may be one of the last times you have sex where you don't have to worry about a sneaky cat attack in the middle of it."

I kissed him, sucking on his lower lip until he made a low moan. "We'll get Kevin a cat friend. Someone to occupy him so I have plenty of time to make you scream and cum until you can't think straight."

Tristan grinned at me. "That, Shepherd Hayes, is an excellent idea."

Please enjoy an excerpt from Book Three in the Temptation Series, "Taste"

TEASE

Jack

I CLOSED MY LAPTOP AND LEANED BACK IN MY OFFICE CHAIR, rubbing at my temples. I'd found it impossible to concentrate. Not because Connor was in my house, but because I hadn't slept well last night.

You didn't sleep well because you kept picturing Connor's gorgeous body lying in the bed with you. Maybe your dick sandwiched between those tight ass cheeks of his while you stroked his cock and he begged you to let him cum.

I pushed back my chair and stood, ignoring the temptation to walk down the hallway to the library and "check" on the progress of the bookshelves. Connor didn't even realize I was home. Not that I had to hide away in my office while he worked, but it was better... safer, if I didn't see him.

Feeling restless, I walked to the window and stared out into the back yard.

"Holy fuck," I muttered.

Connor was in the back yard. He'd set up his table saw in the flat grassy area of the yard about ten feet from the pool and he was currently measuring a plank of wood. It was a hot day and he'd stripped off the "Hayes Carpentry" work shirt he normally wore. I stared at his upper body in the white tank top. I was in good shape and worked out on the regular, but Connor's upper body was jacked with muscle and beyond sexy.

I was tempted to unzip my pants and yank on my own dick as I watched Connor bend down and pick up a piece of wood, his jeans clinging to his ass.

"Fuck," I said, "what I wouldn't give to tap that ass."

"You shouldn't swear in front of little kids."

The voice coming from behind me made me scream and clutch at the windowsill before I whipped around. I stared at the tiny human standing in the doorway of my office. She looked to be around five or six and her blonde hair was pulled away from her face in two pigtails. She wore a pink t-shirt and green shorts and sandals that lit up as she walked toward me.

"When my daddy swears in front of me, he has to put a dollar in my piggy bank." The little girl stopped in front of me, staring expectantly at me.

"Who are you?" I said.

"I'm Eva. Who are you?"

"Jack," I said. "How did you get in my house, Eva?"

"Uncle Connor had a key," she said. "Do you have any cookies? I'm hungry."

"I don't have any cookies," I said.

Her face dropped and feeling weirdly guilty, I said, "Cookies are bad for you."

She shrugged. "Only if you eat a lot of them."

She walked over to my desk and ran her hand across the top of it. "I like your desk. It's shiny."

"Thank you."

"I like your whole house," she said. She glanced at the open doorway. "Uncle Connor said I had to stay in the library because I'm not supposed to be here, but I got bored, and I had to pee."

"Did you find the bathroom?" I said.

"Yes. Your tub is really big. I could go swimming in it." She moved to the bookshelf behind my desk and stared up at the books. "You have a lot of books."

"I like reading," I said.

"Me too. Have you read any Beverly Cleary books?"

"No," I said.

She frowned. "They're really good books. I'll bring you one of mine so you can read it. I'm only in kindergarten but my teacher said I read at a second grade level. Auntie Angie says it's because I'm really smart."

She joined me at the window, staring up at me. "I heard Uncle Connor telling Daddy that you're rich. How much money do you have?"

"A lot," I said.

"I have thirty dollars in my piggybank." She grinned at me. "Uncle Connor swears a lot when he's watching football. Auntie Nora says he's gonna pay for my college education all by himself. But I'm gonna use the money to buy myself a Barbie car. Did you know it drives just like a real car? It has a gas pedal and a brake and everything. Avril in my class got a Barbie car for her birthday. She let some of the kids drive it at her birthday party, but she said I couldn't. She said I would drive it too fast and crash it."

"Would you?" I said.

She thought for a minute before nodding. "Yeah, probably. Uncle Shepherd says you have a lot of cars. My favourite car is the Ford Mustang Shelby GT500. What's yours?"

"Mine is -"

"Eva!" Connor came rushing into the office. There was sawdust clinging to his face, and he was wearing his work shirt again.

"Eva, I told you to stay in the library while I was outside cutting the wood." Connor scooped her up in his arms.

"I had to pee," Eva said.

He gave me an apologetic look. "Sorry, her dad had a work emergency, and I was the only one who could pick her up from school. He'll be here in, like, five minutes to pick her up."

"Jack has a really big tub," Eva informed him. "I could go swimming in it." She gave me a smile meant to charm. "If I brought my bathing suit, could I go swimming in your tub?"

"Eva, you're not -"

"I have an actual pool you can swim in," I said.

Her eyes widened. "You have a pool?"

"I do."

Eva squealed with excitement before wrapping her little arms around Connor's thick neck. "Uncle Connor, can I come here tomorrow after school and go swimming in Jack's pool?"

"No, honey. I'll be working while I'm here, and you can't go swimming by yourself."

Eva sighed. "But I've never swam in a real pool before, just the stupid lake."

"You're welcome to come by on Saturday and take her swimming," I said.

Connor blinked at me. "Oh, uh…"

"Yay!' Eva shouted. "I'm gonna wear my purple bathing suit and bring Mr. Perkins so he can go swimming too!"

"Are you sure about this?" Connor said to me.

Eva cut him a look. "Uncle Connor, don't ruin this for me."

I burst out laughing and even Connor grinned as Eva clapped her hands. "I'm gonna swim in a pool!"

Connor's phone buzzed and he pulled it out of his pocket. "Your dad is here to pick you up, honey."

"Okay. I'll see you on Saturday, Jack," Eva said, her little face beaming with happiness.

"Hold on," I said and took my wallet out of my pocket as I joined Connor and Eva. I took out a dollar bill and held it out to Eva.

She took it from me and said, "You owe me two dollars."

A puzzled look on his face, Connor said, "What's this about?"

"Jack swore in front of me," she said.

"Only once," I said.

"Nu-uh, you said two bad words." Eva slung her free arm around Connor's neck, the dollar bill I'd given her held tightly in the other hand. "Jack was looking out the window and he said, 'fuck, what I wouldn't give to tap that ass'. Ass is a swear word too."

My face turned the colour of crimson and so did Connor's. Eva stared at both of us. "Why are your faces so red? You look funny."

I didn't – couldn't – reply as Eva said, "Ass is a swear word, right, Uncle Connor?"

"Yeah, Eva." Connor was looking everywhere but at me.

My face on fire, I snagged another dollar bill from my wallet and held it out wordlessly to Eva.

"Thank you, Jack," she said as she took it from me. "It was a pleasure doing business with you today."

Connor made a weird and muffled choking sound before spinning around and striding toward the door. "I'll take Eva to her dad and then get back to work."

ABOUT THE AUTHOR

Evelyn Bloom writes bold and sexy M/M romances that always end in happily ever after.

When not writing, her free time consists of reading, embroidering naughty art, and watching Netflix. She has a serious addiction to lip balm, nineties boy bands, and learning curse words in other languages.

For more information about Evelyn, check out her website at

www.evelynbloom.com

facebook.com/authorevelynbloom

instagram.com/authorevelynbloom

bookbub.com/authors/evelyn-bloom

amazon.com/Evelyn-Bloom/e/B092XD2NPY

ALSO BY EVELYN BLOOM